THE BARKS & BEANS CAFE
MYSTERY SERIES

ROAST DATE

THE BARKS & BEANS CAFE MYSTERY SERIES: BOOK 7

HEATHER DAY GILBERT

Roast Date

Series: Gilbert, Heather Day. Barks & Beans Cafe Mystery; 7

Subject: Detective and Mystery Stories; Coffeehouses—Fiction; Dogs—Fiction Genre: Mystery Fiction

Author Information & Newsletter: http://www.heatherdaygilbert.com

FROM THE BACK COVER

Welcome to the Barks & Beans Cafe, a quaint place where folks pet shelter dogs while enjoying a cup of java...and where murder sometimes pays a visit.

After much cajoling, Macy gives in to her neighbor, Vera, and agrees to come to her book club's Christmas party so she can share about the cafe. While public speaking isn't Macy's thing, she wants to brighten Vera's lonely holiday season...and she can sell a little house blend on the side.

When a lively book discussion spirals into a public roast of the mayor—who happens to be sitting in their midst—things get uncomfortable. Soon afterward, the mayor shows up dead in Vera's bathroom, and no amount of gingerbread cookies or eggnog can restore Vera to the club's good graces. 'Tis the season for Macy to find the murderer, or else Vera might be taking a long winter's nap in a jail cell.

Join siblings Macy and Bo Hatfield as they sniff out crimes in their hometown...with plenty of dogs along for the ride! The Barks & Beans Cafe cozy mystery series features a small town, an amateur sleuth, and no swearing or graphic scenes. Find all the books at heatherdaygilbert.com!

The Barks & Beans Cafe series in order:

1

Elvis crooned "Here Comes Santa Claus" over our cafe speakers as I draped thick pine garland along an oversized front-facing window. My barista Bristol sang along, centering a lit wreath in the one I'd just decorated.

She stopped her singing long enough to say, "I just love Christmas. Let me tell you, I'm seriously going to deck some halls in a few weeks for Mom's wedding—you know I'm basically her wedding planner."

"Given that gorgeous gold velvet dress she chose for me, I like the way things are headed."

Bristol's mom was my close friend Della Goddard, and, after a whirlwind two-month romance, she and English professor Farrell Emerson were getting married. She'd asked me to be her maid of honor, and I was glad to support her as she took this next step in life. Della's first husband had died young, and though she'd grieved him for years, Farrell had come along and reminded her she still had plenty of love to offer—and to receive.

Bristol nodded, and her magenta hair, which had previously been a glossy shade of brown, curtained her apple-shaped cheeks. "Mom's practically glowing these days. I've honestly never seen her so happy."

"I'm glad she'll have Farrell around when you go off to college next fall, since I know she'll miss you terribly." I plugged in the lights on the garlands, which gave the cafe a warm glow. "*Now* it's starting to look a lot like Christmas." I threw a triumphant glance at the nearly empty decoration bins. "I'll stack these and take them back to my attic," I said. "You can head on home. Thanks so much for dropping in today—I'm glad we closed so we could get this done."

"These past few Sundays haven't been very busy, anyway." She grabbed her purse and headed for the door. "See you tomorrow."

After grabbing the plastic bins, I headed for the connecting door linking the cafe to my half of the house. I only used this door when there were no customers around. Although I considered myself a reasonably outgoing person, I did value my privacy, and when that door was open, people could peer directly into my hallway.

As I pulled the door closed behind me, I was greeted by my seated Great Dane, Coal, who was blocking the hallway with his hundred sixty-five pound frame. His huge black tail thumped the wood floor, and his expectant amber eyes met mine.

"I'll give you a treat, boy, but you have to get out of the way first," I said. "I'm heading up to the attic."

At the word "attic," he cocked his head as if he were perhaps familiar with the term. But he didn't budge.

"Out of the way," I said, stepping forward.

He clattered to his feet, sticking by my side as I dragged

the bins toward the stairs. "We can't both fit," I explained. Realizing he might be underfoot because he needed a bathroom break, I headed toward the back door and opened it. He obligingly loped out into the back garden.

I made the trip up and down the attic stairs, then decided to brew myself a cup of coffee. Once that was in hand, I headed out onto the porch to join Coal, since it was an unusually sunny December day. A little extra vitamin D was always a good thing.

The cozy smell of wood smoke drifted on the air as I took a slow sip of coffee. Our Barks & Beans Cafe house blend was everything coffee should be, although I did augment mine with heavy doses of cream and sugar.

I could see my neighbor Vera standing at her mailbox on the sidewalk. She shoved a thick stack of envelopes inside before pulling up the red flag. When she caught sight of me, she threw me a wave, then walked over to my fence. I headed over to greet her, instructing Coal to sit as I did so.

Her short white hair and petite stature always gave her a spritely appearance, and today her outfit looked straight out of L.L. Bean.

"Macy! It's good to see you." She pulled her quilted green vest tighter against some imperceptible chill. "I have the house nearly all ready for book club on Friday. All my reader friends are so anxious to hear you speak about the cafe. Randall will be joining us, too."

Vera had been dating Randall Mathena for several months now, and even though she hadn't referred to him as a "boyfriend" yet, I was positive they were an item.

"I'll be glad to see him again. And I think I'm all ready to discuss *Vanity Fair*." It had been a surprisingly interesting classic, so I was glad I'd agreed to join them this month.

She grinned. "Well, you'll never guess who's leading the book discussion."

"Oh, it's not you?" I'd assumed Vera would facilitate the talk, since the club met in her home.

She shook her head. "Lawsie, no. I'm in charge of refreshments this time. But I had an amazing volunteer—Goldie Keaton, can you believe it?" Her brown eyes twinkled.

I blinked, feeling more than a little intimidated. "You mean the mayor of Lewisburg?"

She bobbed her head. "The very one. Goldie's been in our club a few months, and I have to say she's exceptionally well-read. She went to one of those Seven Sisters colleges—Barnard, I think—and she's offered to lead the discussions from here on out. It's a relief, actually. I always flounder around trying to come up with deep questions, and they seem to come naturally to Goldie."

Something niggled in the back of my mind. "Wasn't there some kind of scandal when she ran for office last year?"

Vera huffed. "Yes, but it was entirely due to that nitwit Emory Gill. If you recall, he was running against Goldie, and he was absolutely committed to making her look bad. She was out for her nightly walk on the Greenbrier River Trail, and some young girl stopped her and asked how far it was to get to the nearest outhouse. Soon after, a retired drug dog out for a walk sniffed Fentanyl in the young lady's backpack, so the owner called the cops. Turns out, the girl was some kind of drug courier from out of state. But Emory made it sound like Goldie had passed her the drugs on the trail. As *if* she would do anything so stupid!" She placed a hand on my arm. "She told me later she was just trying to be neighborly and help someone who seemed in a hurry to get to a bathroom—in fact, she said she felt sorry for the girl, since it was already getting dark and she was walking alone. You know that trail's not lit."

I nodded, since I'd been on the wide trail many times. It had been built on an old railroad grade, so it made for a nice, non-taxing walk. Trees shaded the walkway, and the river ran along one side of it. People regularly rode bikes and even horses on it. But I wouldn't walk it late at night without a friend—and a weapon of some kind.

A sudden *woof* sounded from Vera's back yard. Coal gave a reciprocating bark from my garden, which backed up to Vera's fence. Vera's rescued Labradoodle Waffles was a constant source of both consternation and fascination for Coal, so they "spoke" to each other across their respective boundaries every chance they got.

"Is it just me, or does Coal sound a little friendlier today?" I asked.

Vera laughed. "Possibly, but I'm guessing he's just anxious for you to come back to him. I'd better head inside —I have gingerbread cookies in the oven. I'm going to freeze them, then ice them right before book club." She winked. "I'm cutting them into doggie shapes, to go with your Barks & Beans talk."

Involuntarily, my mouth started to water. I could almost taste the spicy goodness of Vera's locally famed gingerbread cookies. "I can't wait. Oh—and Bristol and Charity are helping me put gift baskets together to give as door prizes. Bo's going to grind several bags of house blend for me to sell after my talk. So I think I'm all set."

She squeezed my arm and gave an excited little hop. "That sounds perfect. Thanks again for finally giving in to my relentless requests to speak. I think you'll find the book club is full of welcoming people."

DECIDING I needed a little more exercise after being cooped up all morning, I put Coal on his leash, and together we walked around the block, then over to the next street.

Once we'd made it halfway down the loop, I caught sight of Matilda Crump standing on her front porch, stringing Christmas lights across her railing. Matilda was older than Vera—nearly seventy, I believed—and she was one of a kind. She used an affected British accent, which she'd adopted after one visit to her now-dead husband's parents in Britain. She held a healthy dose of disapproval for most people, but saved her outright scorn for special cases. Nevertheless, she was one of the most well-informed people in Lewisburg, since she was active in nearly every social circle.

As we approached, I asked, "Could I give you a hand with that, Matilda?"

In spite of her thick glasses lenses, I could tell she was directing a cold stare at Coal. "I'd thank you more to keep that big lug out of my yard." She gave a haughty sniff. "Just pootling around town, are you?"

I had no idea what it meant to "pootle," but that sounded about right. "We are."

She haphazardly twisted lights around the rail. "Are you all set for your big speech?"

I assumed she was referring to my talk at the book club, although it didn't help my nerves to think of it as a "big speech." My wavering voice betrayed me as I answered, "I think so."

She gave a brisk nod. "I heard that Goldie Keaton will be leading the discussion. While she's utter rubbish at being a mayor, I have to admit she does come up with some good questions."

"*Rubbish* is a strong word." I tried to hide my grin.

Without cracking a smile, she retorted, "I don't know what else to call someone who doesn't care for the seniors in her community. Why, last night she flatly refused to join her fellow council members when they went caroling to the Lilac Terrace nursing home. She claimed she couldn't carry a tune, but her neighbor told me what she was actually doing during the caroling hour—entertaining a gentleman in her home. A gentleman who was *not* her husband, I might add. Her neighbor saw him heading out the door."

Coal eased himself into a sitting position, heaving what I could only describe as an exasperated sigh. He wasn't so keen on Matilda's caustic tone, and neither was I.

With absolutely no encouragement, she continued her tirade. "It was Doctor Mark Schneider, that psychologist from Ivy Hill," she explained. "He's been married to my dear friend Lena for over thirty-five years." Her lips flattened. "She'd be gutted if I told her, but what choice do I have? Doesn't she deserve to know of her husband's tomcat ways?"

I gave her an *are-you-serious* look. "I've met Doctor Schneider. He's a kind man. I'd be really careful before you start accusing him of infidelity."

She blew air from her lips. "And what would *you* do if it were your friend, Miss Macy?"

She had me there. When I'd discovered my ex-husband, Jake, had been cheating on me, I'd been taken completely unawares. I supposed it would've been easier in the long run if I'd known about it earlier in the game so I could've confronted him. Instead, he'd up and walked out on me, leaving me and my emotions in a very fragile place. Not to mention my limited finances.

Unwilling to get dragged into the soap opera underbelly of Lewisburg's older generation, I gave a noncommittal shrug. "I'm not sure." After lightly tugging Coal's leash, I shifted to the side as my giant dog rose to his feet. "Well, we'd better get on home. Coal's probably tuckered out."

Matilda gave me a dismissive wave. "I should imagine so. I'll see you on Friday." Her tone seemed more ominous than eager.

I felt a touch of dread for the mayor, who would be walking into a book club that might not be on the friendliest of terms with her, given Matilda's interference. One could only hope Vera's enthusiasm for the party would keep the holiday spirits high.

2

A ll thoughts of Matilda's snooping ways flew to the four winds when I got a call from Bo on my way home. "Could you drop by a minute, sis? I have something important to show you."

I was only minutes away, since my older brother Boaz —"Bo" for short—lived in the house on the other side of Vera's. When our great-aunt Athaleen had died a few years ago, he'd decided to renovate the front half of her house into the Barks & Beans Cafe, then he'd fixed up the back half for me to live in. I'd never been so grateful to move home to West Virginia in my life, given that my divorce had stolen any motivation to stay in South Carolina near Jake and his family.

As I walked up the porch steps to his bungalow-style house, Bo threw open his ocean-colored front door. "Come in, come in," he said, ushering Coal and me inside.

As usual, Bo's feisty cat Stormy acted imperious with Coal. She careened straight toward his leg, giving him a light flick of her paw before tearing up to the top of her cat tower. You'd think a ten-pound Calico would shrink in the face of my towering canine giant, but Stormy was fearless. Coal trotted over and sank to the floor beneath her perch.

"What's this important thing you have to show me?" I asked. "I hope it's something you've cooked me from a fantastic new recipe."

My brother was the cook in the family, whereas I tended to subsist on take-out and freezer fare. Thankfully, he frequently sent food over to me, so I hoped tonight would be one of those times.

He smiled, flashing perfectly-aligned teeth, which had somehow come about with no aid of orthodontics. My teeth were only straight thanks to two and a half years in braces.

Bo's red stubble beard was closely trimmed, and his hair set off his sky blue eyes. It was no secret that several ladies had become regulars at the cafe just to spend time near Bo, as opposed to the shelter dogs we brought in.

But Bo was a one-woman man, and his heart belonged to local animal shelter owner Summer Adkins. As he opened his palm to reveal a blue jewelry box, I gave a gasp.

"What's this?" I fought the urge to snatch it from his hand.

His smile widened. "I'm thinking you can guess."

I gave an excited clap. "It's a ring, isn't it? You're going to ask Summer to marry you!"

He nodded, gingerly opening the box to show me.

The ring sat on a bed of blue velvet. It was a delicate gold band with one large, square diamond flanked by two smaller matching diamonds. They twinkled in the living room lighting.

"It's called a step-cut diamond," Bo said, excited as a

little boy. "I researched all kinds of cuts, and this one reminded me the most of Summer—beautiful in its simplicity."

I gave a mute nod as tears sprang to my eyes. My brother, who'd been cruelly rejected years ago by his fiancée Tara, was finally able to offer his heart—and his life—to someone. And not just *any* someone, but one of the most genuine, loving friends I'd ever had.

"It's perfect," I breathed. "She's going to love it. When are you proposing?"

"I've booked a horse-drawn carriage ride through town the Saturday before Christmas. You and Titan are welcome to join us, if he's visiting then."

My boyfriend, FBI agent Titan McCoy, was indeed coming in from Virginia that weekend. He planned to spend a few days at a cabin outside town before driving up to northern West Virginia to visit with his family. "I'm sure he'd love to," I said, trying to imagine the look on Summer's face when Bo popped the question. It was sweet of him to let us be in on their special moment.

Snapping the lid shut, he headed toward the kitchen. After pulling a storage bowl from a cabinet, he ladled chili into it from a big pot on the stove. "Take this home with you."

"That smells amazing. Thank you." I sidled over to steal a warm piece of cornbread from the cast-iron skillet he'd baked it in. Bo had Auntie A's cornbread recipe down pat. After splitting the piece open and slathering butter along the middle, I took a huge bite and sighed.

"You haven't lost your touch," I said.

"Thanks. Goodness knows I make it all the time." He popped the lid on the chili and turned. "Do you feel ready for the book club talk? I'm hoping you'll send lots of new business to Barks & Beans."

My cornbread started to crumble in my hand, so I quickly polished off the last bites before answering. "I guess I'm ready, although Matilda made it sound like I'll be addressing the United Nations."

He chuckled. "She really takes these community things seriously, doesn't she?"

"As well as the community's personal business." My tone was a little dark, and Bo's eyes snapped up to meet mine.

"Something wrong?" he asked. He didn't miss a thing, which made sense since he'd retired early from being an undercover agent for the DEA. He'd honed his ability to scan rooms—and people—to watch for anything that seemed "off." Not to mention, he was extremely protective of his little sister.

I didn't want to throw a dark cloud over our evening. "She's not bothering me, so it's nothing for you to worry about. She's just unnaturally interested in Mayor Keaton's private life, and they'll both be at the book club party."

"Goldie Keaton?" He shook his head. "Surely she's not involved in something underhanded. All those accusations of her doing some kind of drug drop were proved to be completely unfounded. They were likely cooked up by Emory Gill."

"That's what Vera said, and she trusts her, so that goes a long way in my book. No, Matilda's just been talking with Goldie's neighbor, and she thinks there's some kind of affair going on between her and Doctor Schneider."

As Stormy did a surprise pounce onto Coal's back, Bo shook his head. "Mark Schneider is totally loyal to his wife.

Those two are always out on the town, holding hands and visiting shops and restaurants. Matilda's full of beans."

"It wouldn't be the first time." I picked up my chili bowl, then headed over to slip into my shoes. Coal nudged the kitty off his back before trotting my way, his look brightening. He was longsuffering with Stormy's frisky antics, but after a certain point, she basically wore him out.

I gave Bo a big hug. "Thanks for the food—and for showing me the ring. It's spectacular, bro. She's already head over heels for you, but this'll definitely seal the deal."

For a split-second, a look of hesitancy flickered in his eyes. I hated that Tara had left him so wounded that he'd have even the slightest doubt Summer was going to accept his proposal. But he covered his misgivings with a cheery smile. "I certainly hope so."

Colored lights twinkled along Vera's porch on Friday night as I knocked on her door. Randall opened it, giving me a warm welcome as the smells of gingerbread and vanilla escaped from the house. He looked dapper in a red sweater vest that set off his thick, curly gray hair nicely. He led me through the entryway hallway and into the living room.

Michael Buble's version of "White Christmas" was playing on the speakers I'd set up earlier that day. While I wasn't a techie by any means, I did know how to do a few things, and I was glad the speakers had added some holiday ambiance to the party. I arranged my gift baskets and coffee bags on a side table, then headed into the kitchen to greet Vera.

She was looking fabulous in a green turtleneck sweater dress and a chunky gold necklace, even though she'd tied a cartoony Christmas apron over it. With an excited squeal, she stretched out her arms to give me a hug. "Macy! You look beautiful!"

I wasn't about to explain the tremendous effort it had taken to settle on my clothing for the evening. I'd started out by buying two new outfits I'd later decided didn't fit right, so then I'd tried on at least nine others, taking photos to determine if anything met my criteria of being both comfortable and classy.

After writing off all nine looks as flops, I'd finally settled on a poppy-red blouse and black pants, both of which were at least fifteen years old. I'd straightened my hair and bangs, but since snowflakes had been swirling as I walked over, I was sure that at some point tonight, the dampness would make my wavy hair pouf out in the most alarming of ways.

I should've just asked my barista Milo for clothing tips —his family was among the town's elite, so he was a regular at upscale events like this. If I was ever asked to speak at something again, I'd be sure to tap his insights...or just skip the event and talk Bo into going in my place.

But Vera was looking at me like I'd strung the moon, so I felt vindicated in my efforts. She ladled spiced eggnog out of a punch bowl and handed me a small glass of it. "Some sweet fortification for your talk." She continued speaking as I took my first sip, which was incredible. "Here's our schedule—first, I'll introduce you, then you'll have fifteen minutes to share about the cafe. Then Goldie will take the wheel and we'll have our book discussion. After that, we'll break for food and drinks and you can sell your coffee, then we'll return to the living room to review our agenda for next year and announce the gift basket winners. Sound good?"

I nodded, more than happy to go along with whatever Vera had planned. People were already milling around the living room, checking out the gift baskets and the Barks & Beans Cafe magnets Bristol had designed.

Vera bustled around, pulling appetizers from the fridge and arranging them on Christmas plates on the wide butcher block atop her island. "Now you just go and enjoy yourself, honey," she urged. "I'll just be puttering around in here."

Although Bo was the type to stride into a room and own it, I fell into the skulk-in-the-corners-until-I-can-evacuate category of partygoers. Walking into the packed living room was hardly my idea of "enjoying myself." However, I knew what I had to do, so I stood a little straighter, plastered a smile on my face, and walked toward the hubbub.

Matilda was heading straight toward me, fiercely gripping a tray of crumbly-looking sausage balls. She shot me a harried look and said, "Pish-posh, the snow's starting to pour down." Her heavy boots dropped snow clumps on the rug as she entered the kitchen.

Waffles barked from a room in the back, and I realized Vera must've put her in a crate for the occasion. Randall, who was carrying an armful of coats, leaned toward me. "Waffles is in the guest room. I'm going to close the door once I've stored all the coats in there, but if she starts barking during your presentation, I'll get her and take her outside."

"Oh, that's really not necessary," I said. "I'm sure the door will muffle the noise."

He smiled. "I've got my marching orders, missy." He strode down the back hallway, toward the guest room.

I looked toward the entryway, surprised to see my friend Dylan Butler had come. The art gallery owner was dusting snowflakes from his collar-length brown hair. As usual, he was dressed like someone from the highest intellectual echelons, wearing a turtleneck sweater, corduroy blazer, dark jeans, and leather boots. His dark blue eyes settled on me and he gave me a wide, uninhibited smile that immediately made me feel at ease.

"I thought I'd better show up at one of the most important Christmas parties in Lewisburg," he explained, stepping into the living room. "After all, *the* Macy Hatfield is going to be speaking."

I grinned. "Tell me you didn't get your hopes up. I'm pretty sure I'm going to botch this thing."

Raising one eyebrow, he said, "Just think of it as a business pitch. Make these folks feel like they're missing out if they don't visit the cafe, because they are."

Dylan was single-minded when it came to growing his business, and he was always looking for unique ways to expand the reach of his gallery, The Discerning Palette. I appreciated his dispassionate approach tonight more than ever, because it helped me focus on what was important. This wasn't about how polished I looked or how eloquently I spoke—it was about letting townspeople know what a unique experience they'd have if they visited the Barks & Beans Cafe.

"Thank you," I whispered. Dylan was a good friend to me, although he'd let me know he wished we were more than just friends. But once Titan had walked into my life, all bets were off. The tall FBI agent had completely stolen my heart, and Dylan had the decency to respect that fact.

As the strains of "Jingle Bell Rock" tinkled in the background, a woman tapped Dylan's arm. She gave him an expectant look, so he obligingly began to introduce us. "Macy, this is Rashana Evans—she's a city council member. Rashana, this is Macy Hatfield, the speaker tonight."

Rashana bubbled, "Oh, I'm so pleased to meet you! I've been in your cafe once, but I didn't get to stay as long as I wanted. I think it's wonderful what you're doing for those shelter dogs." She leaned in closer. "And how's that handsome brother of yours?"

"He's doing well." Perhaps I should elaborate that he was very much in love with his girlfriend, given the eager look in Rashana's dark eyes.

"Rashana works at The Greenbrier Resort," Dylan explained.

The Greenbrier was one of my favorite places to visit— from its stately white exterior to its surprisingly vibrant interior, the entire experience of going there felt sumptuous. I tried to visit every spring, so I could savor their color-grouped tulip beds. And I always picked up some handmade maple cream chocolate truffles. "I love that place," I said.

"I'm a part-time wedding planner there." Rashana clasped her hands together. "We're having a Christmas wedding next weekend—white roses, red dresses, greenery everywhere—it's going to be gorgeous." She seemed to lose her train of thought as the mayor stepped inside the living room.

Goldie pulled her snow-flecked hood off and shot us a warm smile. It always jolted me a little to see her dark, short hair, which somehow seemed incompatible with her name. The only Goldie I'd ever heard of was Goldie Hawn.

"Excuse me." Rashana abruptly hurried toward Goldie, as if she had some pressing matter to discuss with her.

Matilda stalked past me, heading over to stand with a woman who was actively shooting black looks at the mayor.

Dylan followed my gaze. "That's Nancy Gill," he said under his breath. "She's Emory's wife—he's the guy who ran against Goldie. I think she was even more upset than he was when he didn't win the vote, and from what I can tell, she keeps busy circulating rumors about the mayor. Every time she comes into the shop, she's got some new story about Goldie's failings."

I was guessing Matilda was about to add fuel to Nancy's fire by spreading the rumor that Goldie was having an affair. Although cheating in marriage was despicable, sharing non-verified information with the intent to destroy seemed equally reprehensible. Realizing someone needed to thwart Matilda, I clenched my jaw and strode toward her.

But Vera sidled over, offering me a large gingerbread cookie that resembled Coal. She'd added the special touch of a red frosting scarf around his neck. "It's almost time for your talk, but you'll have enough time to eat this first," she said. "I want to introduce you to Goldie, too." She walked over and tapped the mayor on the shoulder.

Temporarily distracted from my mission with Matilda, I took a bite of my doggie cookie, but I couldn't stomach anything more before I had to speak. I glanced around, catching sight of a beautiful lady in an armchair. I'd seen her once before, at an oyster roast, and I recognized her as Lena, Doctor Schneider's wife.

She shot a demure glance toward the mayor, but she was gripping her glass of eggnog so hard, her knuckles had gone white. Despite her ruby and diamond rings and her designer clothing, it was clear she was incredibly unhappy.

The angst in the living room was thick enough to cut as Goldie walked my way. She stretched out a hand to shake mine, but her smile didn't quite reach her eyes as she said hello. Given Matilda's gossip first, verify later campaign, I was pretty sure I could guess why.

3

"What a delight it is to meet you, Macy." Goldie looked relieved to be speaking to me, as if I might be one of her only allies at the party. "I've heard so much about you from Vera." As she wrapped an arm around Vera's shoulder, she had to lean down. Goldie was tall—she might've even been six feet. She looked businesslike in her button-up shirt, pants, and low-heeled boots. I could see how some might find her intimidating, but since I'd grown up with a taller brother and Titan was six-foot-five, her height didn't faze me.

"And you." While I wasn't really sure if Goldie was a great mayor by any means, I felt sorry she had to endure such a high level of animosity at the book club.

Vera told Goldie, "I'll bring you a glass of eggnog." She patted my arm. "Are you ready to get started?"

Despite my sudden urge to run home and let the party go on without me, I nodded.

Vera gave an impressive whistle, bringing conversations to a standstill. "Everyone, find yourself a seat. It's time to begin." After introducing me, she headed into the kitchen.

I placed a hand on the coffee display table for support. After taking a deep breath and forcing my lips into a smiling position, I began to share how Bo had cooked up the idea for the Barks & Beans Cafe so I could do what I loved, which was to hang out with dogs all day.

Vera slipped in, bearing a glass of eggnog that she quietly handed to Goldie. Then she sat down on the loveseat next to Randall.

The mayor sipped at her eggnog, her eyes closed in delight while I continued.

I told a few funny stories from our childhood with Aunt Athaleen, then I realized Vera was tearing up. She was one of the few people who knew that our parents had died in a sudden creek flood and that Auntie A had stepped in and adopted us.

Trying to keep it together in the face of Vera's emotions, I turned the topic back to the cafe. I explained how Bo and I worked closely with the shelter to rotate dogs through the Barks section. When I revealed the number of dogs that had been adopted since we'd opened our doors, several people gasped, and one lady even clapped.

I shared that Bo ordered special shipments of our house blend beans from Costa Rica, since he'd made connections there when he was vice president of Coffee Mass in California. The book club perked up when I elaborated on the notes in our house blend coffee—light citrus and brown sugar—and Dylan gave me the kind of supportive smile that told me I was moving along the right track.

Hoping to build on my momentum, I held up one of our gift baskets to display what was in it—gift cards from local shops, a Barks & Beans tumbler, Charity's chocolate peppermint patty cookies, and two bags of Barks & Beans Cafe house blend coffee.

When I concluded, the club members gave me a round of applause, which I found surprisingly satisfying. I sank into a nearby chair, feeling grateful for the opportunity Vera had foisted upon me. She gave me a grin before slipping back into the kitchen.

Tapping at the well-worn blue hardcover in her hand, Goldie said, "Let's discuss *Vanity Fair*, shall we?"

She gave a quick rundown of Thackeray's life and relationships, which I found fascinating. I'd read the novel last month, and I'd been surprised at the depth of human insight Thackeray had brought into his tale, even though his satirical bent had also shaped the story.

Goldie expounded on the bigger themes in *Vanity Fair*, and I found myself sinking into her literature lesson as I would a gripping documentary.

"Any theories as to why Thackerey had Becky Sharp—clearly his main character—have an illicit affair with Lord Steyne?" she asked.

Lena Schneider piped up in her clear voice, "I just feel there's no excuse for that kind of thing. Those who have affairs should be brought to light, plain and simple, to save everyone the heartache of finding it out secondhand."

Goldie looked slightly confused, but she gave a slow nod. Matilda let out an unconcealed snort. I got the uneasy feeling that the discussion was about to go off the rails, but Goldie plunged ahead. In hopes of showing we weren't all hostile, I took a stab at her next question, but only got it partially correct.

When Goldie asked which fatal flaws kept Becky Sharp from being a hero—since the book's full title was actually *Vanity Fair: A Novel without a Hero*—it was Nancy's turn for a smart remark.

"Perhaps she ignored waste issues on a public walking trail." Her eyes narrowed. "Or maybe she failed to allocate enough funds to update a water treatment plant."

The discussion of *Vanity Fair* had clearly turned into a public roast of the mayor, spearheaded by the bitter Nancy Gill. I threw a wild glance toward the kitchen, wishing Vera would return or Randall would speak up and put the kibosh on all the negativity.

Thankfully, Rashana intervened. Although her voice was southern-sweet, her eyes flashed a clear warning that Nancy had stepped into the danger zone. "This isn't helpful, honey."

Nancy's lips tightened and she dropped her hostile gaze, fidgeting with her purse. I stole a glance at Matilda, whose foot was anxiously tapping as she tried to feign interest in the Christmas tree. I wanted to tell her, "Now see what you've started," but I supposed she wasn't entirely to blame for Nancy taking such liberties in a book club discussion. The woman was obviously a sore loser—on her husband's behalf.

To nearly everyone's relief, Vera poked her head in, and I got the feeling she'd caught the tail end of the conversation. She spoke cheerily into the awkward silence. "I have some meatballs ready, if you all are ready for some refreshments," she said. "Macy will be selling her coffee now, if you wanted to pick up a bag or two for Christmas gifts. After that, we'll announce the gift basket winners."

Goldie shot her a grateful smile. "That sounds wonderful. Thank you all for your participation tonight. I tallied your email votes, and our book for next month will be *Where Angels Fear to Tread* by E.M. Forster."

"I guess she knows a thing or two about tallying votes," Nancy said, loud enough for anyone around to hear.

Hoping this whole thing would blow over, I began straightening magnets on the basket table. I could hear the people behind me moving into the kitchen. By the time I turned, Goldie was making a beeline upstairs. I couldn't blame her—if something like that had happened to me, I would've run straight out the front door.

Matilda moseyed over to the table, grabbed a bag of coffee, and began sniffing at it. Hoping against hope she wouldn't press her actual nostrils to the bag, I tried to distract her. "The beans are fresh from Bo's supplier in Costa Rica," I said. "He ground them just this morning."

She plopped the bag back on the table and said, "I prefer tea." Glancing around, she asked, "Have you seen the mayor? Did she go home?"

Frustrated at Matilda's determination to take potshots at Goldie, I responded sharply. "Now, why would she want to go home, I wonder?"

When Matilda's eyes widened, I reluctantly added, "I saw her heading upstairs—probably to use the restroom."

That seemed to shut down her questions. She clamped her mouth shut and headed for the kitchen.

Lena Schneider stepped up to the table next, acting like she hadn't heard my snippy remarks toward Matilda. "I'd like a couple bags of your house blend," she said quietly. She didn't quite meet my gaze, and I figured she felt bad about her earlier outburst.

I tried to put her mind at ease by making conversation. "I hear the Ivy Hill Center is doing well. We hope to visit the drug rehab wing with some shelter dogs in January."

She gave a slow nod. "The rehabilitation program has really been successful. Mark says those who graduate from it have some of the lowest relapse rates in the state." A smile crept onto her lips as she spoke of her psychologist husband. I found it difficult to believe their marriage was in such dire straits that he would cheat on her with the town mayor—and in plain sight for the whole neighborhood to see, no less.

"He and Katie have really turned that place around." I slipped a magnet into her stamped paper gift bag. "I remember what it was like before, when it was a spiritual healing center. It seemed kind of dead." Katie Givens was a masseuse who had partnered with Doctor Schneider to buy the building and property, then together, they'd retooled the center to better meet the needs of the community.

I saw a shadow of distrust cross Lena's eyes, and I realized that mentioning Katie hadn't been an encouragement —maybe more like a mistake. "Yes, he's put in long hours tweaking things at the center," she said thoughtfully. It was almost as if she were just realizing that Katie, who was admittedly a tall, younger blonde, worked closely with her husband.

She took her gift bag and darted toward the kitchen. Nancy ended her conversation with Dylan and hurried after Lena, presumably to compare notes on the mayor.

Dylan headed for my table, concern in his eyes. "Everything okay?"

I nodded. "She just seems to be having a rough day."

His lips pinched together. "I promise, book club isn't normally this sensational. I don't know what's gotten into people. It's supposed to be a Christmas party, for crying out loud."

Suddenly, shrieks sounded in the kitchen. Out of nowhere, Waffles came zipping into the living room.

With her tail wagging, the blond doodle charged straight toward me. Dylan, who was none too fond of dogs, stepped back as Waffles reared up and placed her front paws smack in the middle of my blouse.

Randall wasn't far behind. "Waffles, get down!"

Vera shouted, "What's she doing?" from the kitchen. She was probably guarding the food from her rambunctious dog.

"She's okay," I shouted back. Easing both of Waffles' paws into my hands, I lowered her back to the floor, then scratched behind her ears until Randall could grab her collar.

The older man was flustered. "I'm so sorry. I don't know how in the world she got out of that crate. There's no way she could shift open the latch on her own."

Vera hurried in, carrying a retractable lash. "Would you mind walking her, Randall? Maybe she needs to go out."

"Not at all. I'll just grab my coat and boots from the back closet."

"I'll take her into the guest room to wait on you," Vera said. She shook her head. "I'm going to check that latch, too."

As she led Waffles away, Dylan gave me an embarrassed look. "I'm so sorry I didn't help, but I didn't know what to do."

I chuckled. "Hey, I'm the dog whisperer around here, remember? And Waffles and I go way back. She was just coming in to say hello."

We continued to talk for a little while. A knock sounded on the front door, so Dylan walked into the entryway to open it.

Cold wind swirled into the living room as Doctor Schneider stepped inside and stood on the rubber mat. The psychologist had long white hair and round glasses, and, given his rotund stomach, he resembled Santa Claus without a beard. He seemed so cheery, you couldn't help feeling he was trustworthy, which must come in handy in his line of work. People wanted to talk to him—shoot, he'd even gotten *me* to open up more than I'd planned to, when I'd once snooped around at Ivy Hill.

"I've come to pick up Lena," he said. "The snow's falling heavier, and since we live outside town, I wanted to get her on home."

"I'll let her know," I offered, admiring how concerned he was for his wife's safety. I headed into the kitchen and found Lena sitting at the table, talking with Rashana.

I smiled at Lena. "Your husband is here to pick you up. He said it's snowing worse."

A smile formed on her lips, but it quickly faded as Matilda took a long, loud sip of eggnog, then forcefully set her glass on the counter.

I whipped around toward Matilda, and, forgetting my manners, I spat out, "Be careful or you'll break something."

As Lena made her way into the living room, Vera came down the hallway, a confused look on her face. She walked up next to me and said, "I checked that crate latch myself. It's impossible to open from the inside, especially for a dog." She sighed. "Macy, have you gotten some food yet? You have to try my sweet and spicy cranberry meatballs."

Come to think of it, my appetite had returned, now that my talk was over. "I haven't, but I'll get some, thank you."

Once I'd stacked cheese and crackers, meatballs, and veggies and dip on my plate, I joined the others in the living room. Vera announced the gift basket winners, who turned out to be Goldie and Lena.

"Doctor Schneider already picked up Lena, and Goldie must've headed home, too," Rashana said. "I can take Goldie's to her tomorrow, since the council will be meeting in the afternoon." She grinned. "Though I won't say I'm not going to be tempted to swipe those peppermint patty cookies."

After discussing club plans for the weeks ahead, which included an impressive number of community service opportunities, Vera dismissed everyone to retrieve their coats from the guest room. Randall had returned to the kitchen, so I assumed Waffles was once again safe in her crate.

Still looking a little sheepish, Dylan came over to say goodbye. "I really am sorry I didn't stop the dog from jumping up on you," he said. "That wasn't very valiant of me. Could I make it up to you with dinner at the French restaurant?"

I loved the locally-sourced steak at that place, so it was hard to refuse. But I knew something like that would hit Titan like a low blow, even if Dylan and I were only friends. "Thanks, but I don't think that's a good idea."

He gave an understanding but slightly despondent nod. "Sure, I understand. See you around, Macy."

Once he'd slipped into his peacoat and headed into the front entryway, Vera came over to me. "That boy's besotted with you, dear. I think you're the main reason he came tonight. It's too bad, because you're already very much taken, aren't you?" Vera was a huge fan of Titan, and I couldn't say I blamed her.

"Definitely."

She clasped her hands. "Maybe we can look for a good girl to set Dylan up with."

Randall had headed toward the back of the house. "I'll stick around and help you clean up," I offered.

Although Vera protested, she was clearly worn out, so she finally gave in. Together, we started tidying up the trash and loading glasses in the dishwasher. Randall emerged from the guest room with Waffles, who started sniffing around the chairs for scraps.

Suddenly, the dog's ears raised and she darted into the entryway. Nose pressed to the floorboards, she charged up the stairs. A moment later, she started barking frantically.

"What's going on?" Vera asked. All three of us hurried upstairs, only to find Waffles standing by the closed bathroom door, her head cocked.

"Is someone still here?" Vera asked.

Randall shook his head. "Dylan was the last to go, though I noticed there was an extra coat left behind."

"How could someone forget their coat in weather like this?" I asked. As prickles ran up my neck, I gave the door a tentative knock. "Anyone in there?"

When no one answered, I tried the knob. "Locked," I said.

Vera hurried into her bedroom, rummaging through a drawer until she found a straightened paper clip. "This will pop the lock—it's one of those cheap push-button contraptions." She did so, then slowly pushed the door open.

She gasped and gripped the doorframe. Goldie was lying in a heap on the floor, a broken glass of spilled eggnog beside her. The bathroom window was wide open, and snow was drifting in.

The mayor's face was far too pale, and there was a trace of foam on her lips. Vera crouched by Goldie's side, checking her neck for a pulse. After a moment, she shot us a horrified look and whispered, "I think she's dead."

4

Waffles started pacing and whining. Randall offered, "I'll take Waffles out back. She doesn't need to be standing around up here." It was sweet how he was looking out for Vera, who was obviously upset. He took the reluctant dog downstairs.

Knowing I needed to keep a level head, I said, "Bo knows CPR. I'll run next door and get him." Maybe Vera was mistaken and Goldie was still alive, although that didn't seem likely.

I headed to the front door and pulled my boots on. There was no time to grab my coat, so I stepped outside and raced toward Bo's front porch. The freezing air seemed to suck the air from my lungs.

I gave a few frantic bangs on his door, and he opened it with a worried look. "What's—"

"The mayor's on the floor and might need CPR," I wheezed.

Bo didn't wait around. Before I could catch my breath, he'd stepped into shoes and launched into a full-out run that nearly knocked me down. After jumping his bottom steps, he tore toward Vera's front yard.

I followed as quickly as I could. When I stepped into the warm house, Christmas music was still playing, at total odds with the somber scene upstairs. I clambered up to find Vera sitting in a hallway chair while Bo rechecked Goldie's vitals. "There's no pulse," he reported.

"That's what I thought." Vera looked like she was about to pass out, so I grabbed a washcloth, wet it with cold water, and placed it on the back of her neck. "You might want to lie down, or at least put your head between your knees," I suggested.

Once she'd lowered her head, I took stock of the bathroom. "We should probably close the window since it's letting heat out," I said. As I dodged broken glass to pull it shut, I nearly slipped on a puddle of eggnog. Suddenly putting two and two together, I shouted, "Stop!"

Bo, who was still hunched over Goldie, froze in place. "What?"

"Don't do CPR! She might've been poisoned with that eggnog. It could still be on her lips."

"Good point." Vera's voice was muffled against her legs, so I hurried out to check on her. Waving me away, she said, "I'm doing some better now, dear."

The shadow of a smile crossed Bo's lips as I stepped back toward the bathroom. "I wasn't actually planning to do CPR on a dead person, but thanks for looking out for me, sis." He stood. "I'm going to call Charlie and let him know the situation."

Charlie Hatcher was our local police detective, and he was also a close friend. Since Bo was still plugged in with the DEA, he often shared information with Charlie, and vice versa.

As Bo made the call, Vera straightened into a sitting position and threw another glance at the mayor's body. It was very disturbing to see the mayor lying on the floor, her long legs bent awkwardly in the small space and her arms sprawled so that some of her fingers—which looked a little blue at the tips—touched the toilet. While I supposed a tall person might fall to the floor like that, the whole scenario looked a little unnatural, almost like she'd been arranged.

Vera's face seemed to be losing color, so I suggested that I could walk her downstairs. She gave a slight nod. As she gripped the wooden banister, I slipped my hand under her free arm. She was obviously shaken, and I didn't want her taking a tumble down the stairs in her shock.

"Thank you." Her voice wavered. "I was so looking forward to this Christmas party, but nothing went smoothly. From Waffles running out to Nancy cutting loose on the mayor to Goldie lying dead in my bathroom, I don't know how it possibly could've gotten worse."

"So you did hear Nancy's diatribe," I said. "Well, on the somewhat bright side, at least all your guests were gone when we found Goldie. Plus, your food was delicious—especially those cute doggie cookies and your cinnamon eggnog."

She sat down on the couch and frowned. "Do you really think Goldie might've been poisoned with my eggnog? I'd never forgive myself."

Bo jogged down and sat next to her. "Let's not jump to conclusions. We won't know how she died until they check her out. It's possible she had a heart attack."

"But she's so young—in her early sixties," Vera said.

"Unfortunately, these things can happen suddenly," he said.

When the doorbell rang, Bo headed over to answer it. Detective Hatcher walked in, clapping Bo on the back in a brotherly fashion before giving Vera a respectful nod. Then he motioned for a couple of paramedics and police officers to follow him upstairs.

Vera buried her face in her hands. Randall thankfully returned, without Waffles this time. He sat down in the space Bo had vacated.

"I've put her back in the crate," he said, giving Vera's back a soft pat. "I think she's burned off most of her nervous energy for now."

"If only it were that easy to burn off mine," Vera said. "I'm really on edge."

"How about I make us some hot water for tea?" he asked.

"That would be wonderful. I'd better have some of that lavender honey tea—no caffeine right now." She turned to Bo and me. "What would you two like? I have chamomile, lavender honey, and of course some regular black tea."

It was just like Vera to offer refreshments the moment she recovered from a near-fainting experience.

Bo sounded relieved to see her acting more herself. "I'd love some black tea," he said.

"The lavender sounds good." I stood. "I'll help you with it, Randall."

He shook his head. "Oh, no. It's no trouble. I just appreciate you all being here for Vera."

We sat in silence, listening to the activity upstairs, then Detective Hatcher came tromping down to join us.

"The paramedic has declared death. I talked with Goldie's husband, Gary, who's in Louisiana on business, and he said Goldie had no pre-existing health conditions. Then I called the state medical examiner, and he requested we send Goldie's body on to Charleston for an autopsy, since they have to treat this as a suspicious death."

Vera blanched. "Are you saying my bathroom is a crime scene?"

The detective respectfully lowered his voice. "We will have to take photos and gather evidence before you can use it again. I'm sorry, Vera."

"Good lands," she said under her breath.

The detective continued, "I'll be letting Cully Stone know about this—he's the city manager, so the town won't be leaderless. In fact, Cully handles more things than the mayor. He'll have to inform the council members about Goldie, then he'll suggest a deputy mayor."

I leaned forward, wishing I could be more helpful. "I was going to mention that I'd noticed Goldie hightailing it upstairs after our book discussion. I was getting ready to sell coffee at that table there." I pointed to the side table, where only a couple of bags of coffee were left. Bo gave me an approving nod, probably calculating how many bags I'd sold.

"Did you see the mayor come down again?" Detective Hatcher asked.

"I didn't. I was talking with a friend, then the dog got loose, then I headed into the kitchen to get some food. I wasn't really paying attention to the stairs."

"Did you notice what time she went upstairs?" he asked.

I had to think a moment. "No, but I'd guess around forty minutes before the party broke up."

"The last person left around 8:45," Randall offered, bringing in two mugs of tea. He handed Vera the blue one and said, "Be careful, it's hot." He glanced at the detective. "Would you care for some tea?"

Detective Hatcher was all business. "No, thank you." Turning back to me, he asked, "You're saying she went into the bathroom around five after eight, unless she made a stop in another room first?"

I nodded.

Vera said, "My other upstairs doors were closed. Besides, Goldie had been here many times before. She knew right where the bathroom was, and she was far too well-mannered to go barging into a closed-off room." She blew on her tea and took a small sip.

Randall handed me the second mug, then went back to retrieve Bo's.

"Did Goldie wear a coat or bring any other belongings tonight?" the detective asked.

Vera gave a forlorn nod. "I think she wore a red, water-proof-style coat." She glanced around, then pointed to the blue hardcover sitting on Goldie's chair. "And she brought that book over there—she was leading the discussion tonight."

Randall, who'd just handed Bo his mug and settled onto the couch with his own, piped up. "I noticed a red coat sitting on the bed in the guest room. That must be hers."

Sensing that Randall wanted to stay nearby to offer Vera moral support, I stood. "I'll show you to it, detective."

Bo followed us as we headed for the guest room. When

we entered it, Waffles raised her head from a pillow in her crate and gave me a hopeful look.

I crouched down next to her. "We'll all be leaving before long," I explained. "But you'll have to stay in there until then."

Detective Hatcher's hazel eyes twinkled. "Do you always talk with dogs, Macy?"

Bo answered before I could. "She's gotten good at it." He pointed to the only coat remaining on the bed. "That has to be Goldie's."

I nodded. "It's a red waterproof coat, like Vera said."

The detective donned gloves and picked it up, revealing a black leather purse tucked beneath it. "I wonder if that's hers, too."

"I'll check with Vera." Bo jogged out toward the living room.

The detective rummaged through Goldie's coat pockets, turning up nothing more than a cough drop and a tissue. Bo returned, saying that Vera did recall seeing Goldie carrying the black purse.

Slipping his gloved hand into the purse, the detective pulled out a cell phone. When he powered it up, the background was a photo of Goldie and her husband. "This must be hers, all right. I'll have my tech people check it out." He dropped the phone in a plastic bag. After retrieving her leather wallet, he checked the license and nodded. "Hers, too." As he returned the wallet to the purse, he murmured, "Nothing out of the ordinary, it seems."

I took a closer look at the lined coat. "You know, I had a coat just like that a few years ago. It's made for travelers, and it has a couple of inside pockets to hide your wallet and things."

Detective Hatcher said, "I'll check." He patted around until he found the pockets. The first was empty, but he pulled something out of the other.

It was a green, unmarked pill bottle. When he shook it, it didn't rattle. He opened the top and extracted a couple of cotton balls that had been shoved inside. As the loosened pills bounced around, he shook two out onto his palm. "Wait—surely these aren't—"

Bo looked at the pastel-colored pills that strongly resembled Sweet Tarts. His face darkened. "They are."

I was completely at sea. "What do you mean? What are they?"

"Rainbow Fentanyl," the detective said. "You can guess the age demographic these pills would appeal to. I wasn't aware this type had trickled into our area yet." His voice took on a hard edge. "Or that our esteemed mayor was carrying them around to Christmas parties."

5

I was having trouble processing the facts myself. As the detective dropped the pills back into the bottle, I tried and failed to reconcile Goldie's friendly, inquisitive personality with someone who was using drugs. Of course, Bo had told me that opioid use wasn't always as obvious as you'd think, but surely if Goldie had been using, someone on the city council would've noticed.

"Let's keep this detail between ourselves," the detective said. "We'll need to pull prints from the bottle and check into things before making any kind of drug angle public."

"Of course," Bo said.

I shifted, feeling like I was holding out on my distressed neighbor. "We can't tell Vera?"

The detective's look was apologetic. "It's best not to yet, but I promise I'll let her know the moment I find out something definitive."

Vera would be utterly dismayed to discover that drugs had been found in her house, much less that one of her trusted friends was the one who brought them.

I glanced at Waffles. Apparently, the energetic Labradoodle hadn't caught one whiff of the Fentanyl pills that had been sitting right next to her. I supposed only trained dogs sniffed out drugs, like that retired dog on the trail, but I still felt a twinge of disappointment. Would Coal have picked up on their scent?

As we followed the detective out, I had to wonder if the police had dropped the ball regarding Goldie's meet-up with a drug courier. It might not have been accidental, as she'd claimed. Perhaps Emory Gill was right to accuse Goldie of drug running.

In the living room, Randall and Vera were sitting closely on the couch. He'd wrapped an arm around her slender shoulders.

Her voice was charged with anxiety. "Did you all find anything?"

Detective Hatcher held up the coat and purse. "We found Goldie's things, including her phone. We'll be going through them back at the station."

"Of course," Randall said. "Please let us know if there's any other way we can help."

"I'll be in touch," the detective said. "Now I'm going to see how they're coming along in the bathroom." He headed for the stairs.

Bo leaned down to give Vera a tight hug. "I'd better head home, too. I'd imagine you need some serious peace and quiet now, Vera."

She nodded. "Lawsie, but what a night this has been." Grabbing Bo's arm, she added, "Now, you get yourself some of those gingerbread cookies to take home."

He grinned. "I'd be happy to. You want me to bag a few up for you, sis?"

"Please do," Vera said. "And take some of those meatballs, too. I know you like them."

Even in the midst of her Christmas calamity, Vera was reaching out to others and looking out for them. She reminded me of Auntie A in that way.

I jumped up to join Bo, who had pulled out a small container for my meatballs. As I filled it, we shot disbelieving looks back and forth, but said nothing. He was probably deeply concerned about a fresh wave of drugs designed to hook younger people in Lewisburg, as was I. That was the last thing this community needed.

Once Bo had said goodbye and headed out, I gave Vera a hug. "I know it seems like everything went nuts tonight, but really, it was a wonderful party. The food was delicious, my talk seemed to go over well, and we sold quite a bit of coffee."

Vera held up a hand and began ticking things off on her fingers. "But the dog got out, the mayor was ridiculed, then we found her dead in my bathroom. I'm having a little trouble seeing the bright side here."

I shot a helpless look at Randall, wishing I could somehow lift Vera's spirits. He gave me a knowing look and turned to her. "You want to help me put the foods away?"

It was just what Vera needed to propel her into action and out of her funk. "Of course I will," she said, standing. "Macy, thank you again for coming. I know you have every right to blacklist the book club, but we'd be so glad if you wanted to join us again next month."

I'd already watched—and been temporarily traumatized by—the sad movie version of *Where Angels Fear to Tread*, so I had zero plans of reading that particular book club selection. But I offered Vera a genuine smile. "Thank you. I'll think about it." I wondered who would be leading the book discussion, now that Goldie was dead.

S ATURDAY MORNING it was difficult to drag myself out from under the warm quilt layers I'd piled on top of me. When I stepped around Coal's pillow at the end of my bed, he didn't even budge.

"Getting cold, isn't it, boy?" I knew he would resist going out into the snow for as long as he could, but even large bladders like his could only hold so much. "Come on downstairs," I said. "You know you'd better go."

Reluctantly, he plodded down after me, keeping his nose pressed against my thigh all the way. He preferred to stay in physical contact with me as much as possible, which was adorable, at least until he accidentally cut in front of me and made me trip.

I gave his sleek back a pat as he trudged past me onto the porch. "I'll be right here," I announced. The detective was right—I did talk to dogs all the time.

Once Coal had done his business, I brewed some house blend in my French press. Although Kylie was likely prepping machines and grinding beans next door, I was too sluggish to wait around for my coffee.

After drinking two cups and eating a slightly lopsided gingerbread cookie, I headed upstairs to change. I chose a worn gold sweatshirt that always struck me as looking very Hufflepuff, which happened to be my Hogwarts house. Occasionally, I got in the mood to reread the entire *Harry Potter* series, although I doubted I could convince the book club to read them. If they ever did, I'd be sure to attend—I'd even volunteer to lead the discussion.

Again, I thought of Goldie. She had seemed so prepared for last night's discussion, as if she'd put a great deal of time and thought into it. It was a real shame that both Lena and Nancy had ganged up on her.

After turning on the TV to keep Coal company, I headed through the connecting door into the cafe. Summer had just arrived, bringing two dogs with her.

"You ladies want coffee?" Kylie asked from behind the counter. Although our best barista always seemed formidable thanks to the tattoos running up her neck and down her arms, today she looked especially intimidating in her skull sweater and black cargo pants. Everything about Kylie shouted, "Back off," but I'd discovered that deep down, she was as protective and loyal a friend as anyone could hope to have.

Summer swept a strand of honey-colored hair from her eyes. "Yes, please."

"I don't need any," I said, taking the leashes out of Summer's hands. As I walked the dogs toward the Barks section, I tried to wipe the image of Summer's gorgeous engagement ring from my thoughts. If I kept picturing it, I'd start smiling, and then she'd ask me what I was thinking about, since she always read me like a book.

Thankfully, Summer didn't seem to notice anything different. "That gray dog there is called Thistle," she said. "She's extremely friendly, and she likes her water really fresh—otherwise she won't touch it. She wanted to drink straight from the sink at the shelter."

As I leaned down to let Thistle off her leash, her brown

eyes met mine and she almost seemed to grin. "You *are* friendly, aren't you?" I asked, patting behind her soft ear.

The other dog tugged at its leash, anxious to be released. Summer said, "We're calling the reddish dog Copper. She's super quiet and calm—doesn't even bark when the others start yipping away. But, as you can see, she's very overweight for her medium frame at 114 pounds. I guess she swiped a lot of cat food at her previous home. She had to be surrendered when her owner was hospitalized. We're hoping to place her with someone who can take her on long daily walks to get her healthy again."

"Duly noted," I said, letting the sweet but chubby canine join Thistle, who immediately rushed over to join her.

"Those two get along well," I said. "That's not always the case."

Summer nodded. "Don't I know it. Some days I get tired of all the snarling and barking at the shelter, but it's all part of the job."

Kylie walked over and handed Summer a to-go cup of coffee. Summer smiled. "You're a lifesaver," she said. "I'd better get back." She looked more closely at me. "Is something up? You seem a little distant this morning."

"I'll tell you about it tonight," I said. Tonight, like most Saturday evenings, Bo was making a meal for Summer and me, then afterward, we'd "shoot the breeze" for awhile— Auntie A's term for having a good chat.

Summer's brown eyes softened. "Okay, sure." She was probably guessing I was upset about something my ex Jake had done, but, thankfully, he hadn't gotten in touch with me since his last botched visit to West Virginia.

Thistle and Copper continued to play together, systematically exploring one section of the Barks section before moving to another. I tried to keep plenty of toys stocked for our canine visitors, but they wore out quickly. Of course, every day someone had to clean them off for the next day's dogs, which was quite a chore. Once our cafe's income had grown a bit more, I planned to hire a cleaning person. For now, the Barks & Beans employees—and owners—were always on the hook for cleanup duties.

I was just leaning down to pick up a chew bone when a man came into the cafe, talking loudly on the phone. I straightened, watching as he walked up to the counter, where he ended his conversation and gave Kylie his order.

His blustering voice could be heard throughout the cafe as he spoke to her. "There are some strange happenings in this town, don't you think? Have you heard about the mayor?"

I edged toward the low brick divider wall separating the Barks section from the cafe proper. Kylie gave a disinterested shrug, letting him know she had better things to do, before stepping toward the espresso maker. But the obnoxious man rolled right along.

"Yes, indeedy. My wife Nancy was there, where the mayor died. Over at that Vera's house." He turned and glanced toward the Barks section, so I pretended to arrange one of the succulent plants sitting atop the divider wall. He had to be Emory Gill, and he was clearly still smarting that Goldie won the mayoral election. I stole a covert look at him, and was surprised to see he actually resembled a cartoon villain. His nose appeared to have been boxed in more than once, his thin lips were twisted in a veritable snarl, and his small eyes were filled with disapproval.

He continued his rant. "Well, my wife never did care for that Goldie Keaton, anyway. She said the mayor was acting strange from the get-go that night." By this point, a couple of locals had lined up behind him, and they were listening to every word he said.

I couldn't let this continue. He was publicly maligning the mayor's name, not to mention lying about how she'd been acting at the club meeting. And he was ignoring the rule of showing respect for the dead, which I happened to adhere to.

As Thistle gave my leg a friendly nudge, hoping I'd throw her the ball, I gave her a pat on the head. Then I headed out the dog gate and strode toward Emory. I gave him a tight smile, motioning him away from the customer line and toward the pickup end of the coffee bar.

Although he looked a bit hesitant, he trailed after me. When we were out of earshot of the customers, I quietly said, "Hello—Emory, is it?"

I'd hoped the man would follow my lead and lower his voice, but instead, he seemed to get even louder. "That's right. Is there a problem? Miss Hatfield, is it?"

So he knew who I was. "That's right, sir. I was also at the Christmas book club party, and I'm a personal friend of Vera's. I'm sure she'd appreciate it if you weren't discussing Goldie's death in such a public venue as our cafe."

Emory's face turned red. "Why, I never. I come in here for a cup of coffee and this is the thanks I get from the owner?"

Kylie stood behind the counter, gripping Emory's coffee as if she wasn't about to hand it over. She leveled a flat-out glare on him.

Trying to smooth things over since people at the tables

were now watching, I said, "I'm sorry, sir, but it's not constructive to speak ill of the former mayor, especially for the sake of her friends and family." Out of the corner of my eye, I noticed that Bo had emerged from the back room and was walking toward us.

Emory huffed. "I'll take my coffee and go, then. And I won't be back."

"That's a good idea." Bo adopted a wide-legged, aggressive stance behind Emory, his arms crossed in all their muscled glory. His red hair and beard caught the light, making him look like some kind of avenging angel.

Emory's face registered fear, but he spluttered, "Wait'll I tell my friends how I was treated here."

Bo gave him a benevolent half-smile that showed he had the upper hand. "You go right ahead. I've been here much longer than you have, and I'm certain I know all your friends."

Wordlessly, Emory grabbed his cup from Kylie, spilling coffee on the counter. He stormed out.

"What's his problem with the mayor?" Kylie asked, genuinely bewildered. "She always seemed so nice when I ran into her in town. I hate to hear that she died. What happened?"

"I'm sure it'll come out in the news before long." It seemed best to keep the details of Goldie's death quiet until the police gave an official release. But I turned to Bo, who was still watching the door for a possible reappearance. Stepping close to his side, I spoke quietly in his ear. "I do have to wonder—what is Emory's big beef with the mayor? It seems to run far deeper than a simple election loss."

6

I'd just brought Thistle and Copper in from a walk in our side yard when I noticed Rashana was sitting at a table in the cafe, eating a Cuban sandwich. I gave her a wave, and she immediately picked up her things and headed my way.

I smiled. "It's fine if you bring the coffee in, but we don't allow foods in the dog section, I'm afraid." As if proving my point, Thistle jumped up, placing her paws on the divider wall before giving Rashana's half-eaten sandwich a hungry look.

She laughed. "Oh, I didn't even think about that." Placing her food on a nearby table, she carried her coffee mug through the dog gate and stood next to me. "I just wanted to get your thoughts on some things. I know you're close with Vera."

"Of course." I gestured toward a corner table where people in the cafe couldn't hear us. "Please, have a seat."

She took a sip of her coffee. "This cappuccino is delicious, by the way. I'm so impressed with your cafe. I should've come here sooner." She crossed her legs and leaned back. "I wondered if there was any news on Goldie's death. Cully—the city manager—told council members she'd passed suddenly after the book club party and that police were looking into things. But he's been very closed-lipped about how she died, and he has yet to nominate a new mayor."

I wasn't sure what kind of information Rashana was looking for. "I haven't heard anything today," I said honestly.

When Copper nudged her red head against Rashana's leg, she set her mug down, petting the sweet dog as she continued. "I'm just concerned, obviously for Vera, since it sounds like the mayor was found dead in her home. I'm also concerned for the city council, because Cully isn't moving quickly on getting a new mayor in place. He says it's complicated and he wants to wait until things clear up around Goldie's death. But I've had years of experience on the council, essentially doing what Goldie did. I'm happy to step into the position, but I haven't been able to reach Cully since his announce-ment of her death. Is there something he's not telling us?"

I wasn't about to share any details, but I felt sorry for Rashana, because I understood how it felt to be over-looked for promotions when you were the best candidate for the job. It had happened to me twice when I was working at the DMV in South Carolina, and there was nothing more spirit-deflating than having your hard work ignored when higher positions came open.

"I can't really say, but if it puts your mind at ease, I'm checking in with Vera regularly. I'd urge you to continue trying to get hold of Cully to let him know you want to be considered for the mayor position."

"You're right—we'll never know if we never ask, right?" She gave Copper a final pat and uncrossed her legs. "Now, I'd better finish my lunch and get back to the Greenbrier. I'm meeting with a bride and her fiancé today. I wish you all the best with these beautiful dogs."

As she fished hand sanitizer out of her purse, I opened the gate for her to return to the cafe. Thistle trotted over to my side and wagged her tail, eager to play.

A woman with long, dark hair walked into the Barks section and Thistle forgot about me, hurrying over to greet another possible friend.

The woman leaned down and patted Thistle's head. "What a friendly doggie. Aren't you just the sweetest?" she cooed. Turning toward me, she said, "What a beautiful color she is—that sleek gray with the little bits of white on her toes and chest. I wonder what breeds she has in her."

"You'd have to ask my friend Summer at the shelter, if you're interested. She's good about looking up those kinds of facts on her dogs." Maybe the woman was leaning toward adoption. "Were you looking for a dog?"

She chuckled. "Not really, but when I noticed her standing next to you, something compelled me to come over and pet her." Crouching down, she rubbed behind Thistle's ears. "I actually dropped by to order a caramel latte—my friend Jan says they're amazing here."

I nodded. "While you're at it, you should pick up a grilled turkey, bacon, and brie sandwich. Our baker Charity makes them, and they're amazing."

"I'm a vegetarian, but I appreciate the suggestion," she said.

"In that case, the eggplant pesto sandwich might be just the ticket. It's addictive."

Grinning, she said, "I'm impressed. It's hard to find vegetarian options at cafes. I'll go check it out."

As she walked toward the cafe, Thistle let out a prolonged whine. The woman turned and said, "Don't worry, I'll drop in after I eat."

I smiled to myself as I began to play with Thistle and Copper. Making quality matches between humans and dogs was something I could always feel good about.

AFTER WORK, Coal curled up at my feet as I relaxed on the couch, watching snowflakes drift outside the window. Three knocks sounded at my door, so I knew it was Vera. We'd recently worked out that we would each do three knocks to let the other know who it was.

Coal gave a short, hesitant bark, but I shushed him and went over to open it.

Vera stood outside, a bag of cookies in her gloved hand. She looked haggard, as if she hadn't slept much last night, which was no big surprise. She'd wrapped a big scarf around her neck and pulled a purple hat over her ears.

She extended the bag toward me. "I thought you might like the rest of these—they were leftover ones I didn't ice yet."

I gladly took the bag. Several years ago, I'd decided to enjoy holiday treats at the risk of gaining a few pounds, as opposed to abstaining and feeling like I'd missed out on my favorite things. "Thank you. Why don't you come inside and have some hot chocolate or coffee?"

She rubbed her palms along her arms. "Don't mind if I do. I ran over to the church to drop off a casserole for the meal after Denzil Jones' funeral. It was so sad he passed this time of year. I got a little chilled, I think."

Denzil had been a pillar of the community, heading up a coat drive for children at Christmas. A recent bout with pneumonia had weakened him, then his heart had given out. I hated how deaths seemed to pick up in the winter.

As she walked in and knocked snow from her boots, Vera mused, "I wonder when Goldie's funeral will be."

"I'm not sure—I'm assuming the medical examiner hasn't released her yet. What would you like to drink?"

"Hot chocolate, I think." She sat down at the table and heaved a sigh. "I still can't believe we found her lying in my bathroom. It seems so surreal."

I set the kettle on to boil, then took a seat as Coal came over to greet Vera. Once he'd received a little attention, he traipsed back to his pillow in the corner.

Vera looked thoughtful. "I've been racking my brain, but I can't for the life of me figure out what happened to Goldie. I've talked with Gary, and he says she was healthy as a horse. Vitamins were the only pills she took." She tapped her nails, which were a festive shade of red, on the table. "You were in the living room when she went upstairs, right? Did you see anyone go up after her?"

I'd been pondering the same question since yesterday. "I wasn't paying too much attention, since I was talking to people who were looking at the coffee. Let me see...Dylan was standing near the stairs, talking with Nancy a little. Then those two headed into the kitchen, soon after Matilda and Lena did." I had an idea. "Maybe I could ask

Dylan if he noticed anyone going upstairs, since he wasn't standing far from the entryway."

"Good idea," Vera said.

Grabbing my phone, I shot Dylan a text. As I placed Vera's mug in front of her, my phone rang, and I saw it was Dylan.

"That was fast," I said.

"Hi, Macy," he said. "I figured it would be easier to call and explain. The short answer is yes, I saw one person go upstairs." He chuckled. "It was while Matilda was sniffing at your coffee bags. Rashana walked by me and headed upstairs. I heard her knock on the door, then she said, 'Oh, I'm sorry,' like someone was in the bathroom. She came right down and went toward the kitchen. At that point, Nancy came over to talk to me about the possibility of having an art show at Carnegie Hall. I tried to discourage her from it, because, to be honest, her watercolors are...not the best I've seen."

I knew he was being polite, but I could read between the lines. Nancy Gill was no painter, but apparently she considered herself one. "So Rashana was the only one you saw go up?" I asked.

"Yes. Do you think I need to let the police know that?"

While I doubted Rashana was involved, especially since she came downstairs directly after knocking, I said, "You might want to. It's Detective Hatcher in charge, so you could ask to speak to him."

"Will do." He hesitated. "I just wanted to tell you again that I enjoyed your presentation. I remember working with Bo to pick artwork for the cafe." His voice took on an edge. "He was rightfully indignant that your ex had walked out on you."

"The cafe rescued me from a lot of things." I tried to control the wobble in my voice. "I think I was just surviving until I came back here. West Virginia brought me back to life."

"I'm glad you moved here," Dylan said. "It was definitely the best choice for you."

As I ended the call, Vera smiled at me across the table. She placed a hand on mine. "Of course God led you back home," she said. "You and Bo are the best neighbors anyone could hope for. Thank you for helping me out when we found Goldie. I was just so—so overwhelmed at seeing her."

"I was glad I was there."

Once Vera had finished her hot chocolate, I could tell she was too weary to keep talking. "Well, I'd better get on home to let Waffles out," she said. "Thank goodness her crate hasn't malfunctioned again."

As my older neighbor pulled on her purple hat and stepped onto my porch, I felt a strange pang of anxiety on her behalf. It felt like a premonition, as if Goldie's death might not be the biggest problem Vera would have to deal with. But I didn't dare tell her.

"Hang on a minute," I said. When she turned to me, I pulled her into a big hug.

"I just love you," I said.

Her eyes filled with tears. "And I love you like one of my own, honey."

7

Sunday evening, Bo, Summer, and I headed over in the pouring snow to see a play production of *A Christmas Carol* at the Greenbrier Valley Theater. As we took our seats, a man sitting two rows ahead of us turned. His green eyes briefly met mine, then he looked at Bo and Summer. He immediately jumped up and leaned over the empty seats that separated us, extending his hand toward Bo. "You're just the man I've been wanting to see. Come over and chat with me during intermission, okay?"

As the lights began to flicker, I asked Bo who the man was.

"That's Cully Stone, the city manager. He helped me when I was setting up the cafe."

Sometimes it seemed that at least ninety-five percent of Lewisburg must've helped Bo when he set up the cafe, but that was fine by me. That community support had not only helped us get on our feet, but now it continued to funnel business our way. I couldn't understand people who complained about growing up in small towns. That was where you could find your biggest cheerleaders—provided you hadn't burned irreparable bridges along the way.

The play was a welcome escape from my worries about Vera. Both Ebenezer Scrooge and the ghost of Marley had been perfectly cast, and when Tiny Tim said his poignant lines, I was duly moved.

As the lights came on for intermission, Bo headed up to talk with Cully. "Wonder what that's about," I asked Summer.

She was looking lovely in a deep green velvet jacket, and I could tell she'd curled her hair for the occasion. I found it adorable how she and Bo always tried to look their best for each other. "It's anyone's guess," she said. "He hasn't mentioned Cully to me before. Hey—did I tell you that Thistle is getting adopted? This lady called me at the end of the day yesterday and said she wanted to pick her up when we reopen on Monday."

Elated, I said, "It must've been the same woman who was playing with her in the cafe yesterday. I could tell they connected."

Once again, the lights flickered and Bo returned to his seat. I noticed he took Summer's hand in his just before the lights went out.

Afterward, Cully walked back to Bo and said, "Think about it," before heading up the main aisle. Before I had time to ask my brother what that meant, he had already slipped out to pick up his truck.

Summer and I waited several minutes, allowing Bo time to pull up in front of the theater. I knew that, like the gentleman he was, my brother would have the truck's heat cranking to warm us on this cold evening.

I could barely contain the smile threatening to overtake my face as I pictured Bo asking Summer to marry him. When I met her eyes, I wound up staring with a lopsided grin on my face.

She gave me a quizzical look. "What's up?"

I waved a wild hand. "Oh, I'm just excited that Thistle landed in a good home. She was such a friendly dog."

Summer smiled as if that were an acceptable explanation for my weirdness. She looped her arm under mine. "I agree. Now, are you ready to head out into that winter wonderland so we can get home and haul out some of your Christmas decorations? You and Bo are picking out your trees next weekend, right?"

It was endearing, the way Summer frequently referred to my house as "home." Although she rented an upstairs apartment from an older couple in town, it seemed like she belonged in my house as much as I did. In reality, she was already like a sister to me.

"We are—this Friday night." There's no way we'd miss our annual tree farm tradition. When we were kids, Bo and I had been forced to cooperate to choose the best tree for our family. Nowadays, we enjoyed picking them out together, although we still had the occasional disagreement.

True to form, Bo had parked as close as he could to the sidewalk to pick us up. Once we'd climbed into the warm truck, I asked, "So, what was your hush-hush conversation with Cully Stone about?"

Bo pulled out and headed toward home, which wasn't far away. "He wants me to be mayor."

Summer, who was sitting in the front, shouted, "Shut. Up!" and gave him a playful whap on the arm. "I could definitely see you as mayor!"

"I could, too," I said. "But is it something you'd even want to do? I know Rashana Evans is also interested in the position, so you might be stepping into a minefield."

"I honestly don't know." He drove a bit farther, then made a slow turn onto our snowy street. As he pulled to a stop alongside the sidewalk, he said, "Cully assured me that being mayor isn't overly time-intensive, so it wouldn't pull me away from my duties at the cafe. But, like you said, there could be some strife on the council if I step right into the job. I think I want to let Goldie's death sort itself out first, since it's hanging like a black cloud over everything."

"Good idea," Summer said.

The more I considered it, the more I liked the idea of my brother helping steer the city. After all, he'd been a Marine, he was a former DEA agent, he'd been a CEO at Coffee Mass, and now he ran his own business. He had more than enough experience to be a leader in Lewisburg, even if he wouldn't handle as many things as Cully did.

Following my snow-covered solar lights along the path, we tramped up to the back porch. Coal gave us an exuberant greeting, then bounded into the back yard, shoving his nose into the low drifts and frisking like a puppy.

After discarding our wet boots on the indoor mat, I said, "You should consider the mayor position, Bo. You could do some good for the town, and, like you said, it wouldn't be too taxing."

"I'm definitely going to think about it. But I haven't heard anything from Charlie about Goldie's autopsy. If she was murdered, that's going to throw a wrench in the mayoral nomination process, because police will be looking into her work circles."

"True." My phone rang and I saw it was Titan, so I pointed toward the fridge. "I bought a cheese ball, and there are a couple of boxes of crackers in the cabinet."

As Summer and Bo got busy setting out the food, I picked up the call.

"How'd the play go?" Titan asked.

"It was great. I wish you could've come along."

"Trust me, I do, too. I'm up to my neck in work, but I should be able to cut out of here that Saturday I was planning to visit. Any news on the mayor's death?"

I'd given him a brief summary of how we'd found Goldie, but, as per Detective Hatcher's request, I hadn't mentioned anything about the pills in her pocket. "Nothing yet."

"I'm sure you're concerned about Vera. But, given what you've told me about the things she's had to weather in her marriage, I believe she'll make it through this okay. It's not a disgrace to have someone die in your house."

I glanced toward my kitchen counter, where Bo was setting plates out. "But if they find Goldie was murdered, Vera might somehow feel indirectly responsible. She could blame herself."

"Then I'm sure you'll convince her otherwise. You might not be aware of this, but you can be *very* convincing when you want to be." He blew me a kiss on the line. "Though it takes no convincing for me to come to see you soon. I can't wait."

After we'd said our goodbyes, I let Coal back inside, then washed my hands before joining Bo and Summer for snacks. I set out a couple of bottles of sparkling cider I'd tucked away for company.

Summer retrieved three glasses from the cabinet and set them on the counter. "How's your man?"

"Working hard, sounds like." As Summer sat down, I smeared a hearty hunk of cheese ball onto my plate, then grabbed some crackers and grapes on the side. Once I'd poured our cider, I joined them at the table.

"He's still coming in, isn't he?" Bo asked. I could tell he wanted to make certain Titan would be joining us on the horse-drawn carriage ride, but he couldn't give that away.

"Oh, yes." An unexpected flush crept up my cheeks.

Summer noticed and winked. "I'm sure he wouldn't miss it." After taking a sip of cider, she asked Bo, "How well do you know Goldie's husband Gary? Or have you met him?"

Bo nodded, swallowing a bite of food before he answered. "Gary's a good guy. He's been on a couple of fishing trips with our men's Bible study group. I got the impression he and Goldie were happily married. They were always joking around with each other."

I was somehow relieved to hear that. Maybe Matilda's very vocal suspicions that Goldie was having an affair with Doctor Schneider were completely unfounded.

But that raised the question as to why he was at her house when her husband was gone. I could only see one other obvious answer. Maybe he was making some kind of counseling house call.

I didn't know why I was determined to give Goldie the benefit of the doubt, not only about her possible shenanigans with the psychologist, but also about the candy-colored Fentanyl in her coat. Some kind of gut instinct told me she was a good person. Was it simply because she'd been friendly to me? Or was it because her body had looked so unnaturally positioned on that bathroom floor?

On Monday, Summer dropped Copper off in the Barks section a second time. "She's such a great dog, and I have the feeling there's a perfect family out there for her," she said. "If we don't place her today, I do have a foster family willing to take her in, but they're older and less mobile, so they won't be able to exercise her as much as she really needs."

"I'll be her public relations person. Just leave it to me," I said. Surely someone would come in who might be a good fit for the sweet dog.

I had just settled into my routine of tidying up the treat containers on the countertop when Vera walked into the Barks section, looking apprehensive. Once again, she'd wrapped a thick scarf around her neck in a way that partially obscured her face. Maybe she was attempting to stay incognito, even if only subconsciously.

She headed straight toward me. "I hate to bother you at work, but I have a favor to ask," she said.

"You name it." I gave her a quick hug.

She gave Copper's head a pet, then cleared her throat. "Detective Hatcher called me. He said he needs to talk with me about some things, but he's not going to ask me to come to the station. Instead, he'll drop by my house around 12:30 today. Would you possibly be able to come over on your lunch break?" Her hands trembled. "I just need a little moral support. Randall's helping his friend with a patio project all day."

I nodded. "Absolutely. I'll plan to head over around twenty after twelve."

With a sigh, she said, "Thank you."

She didn't have to explain how she was feeling, because I could easily guess. She was alone as she faced this veritable crisis, with no family in sight. Once again, I had the urge to track down her daughter and son and tell them of their mother's situation, but I wasn't sure if they even cared. It made no sense to me, but Vera had never volunteered information as to why they had become estranged.

In the meantime, I was happy to be her backup person. It didn't seem right that, after putting so much energy and effort into making her Christmas party memorable, Vera would be made to feel awful about the entire thing. Surely whatever "things" the detective wanted to talk about wouldn't upset my neighbor further.

8

Bristol, who could easily work both sections of the cafe, was happy to fill in for me while I headed to Vera's place. As I passed her fence, I glanced at her house, which had once belonged to a neighbor we'd known as "Old Man Pettrey." Bo and I couldn't even recall what his first name was. After his death, the house had begun to deteriorate, so we were relieved when Vera had moved in last year and gotten the interior restored.

Then, just this summer, Vera had the house painted a lovely shade of yellow, so it looked like a bright pocket of sunlight set between the evergreen trees lining her yard. The cheery paint, combined with the twinkling Christmas tree lights in the front window, made it difficult to believe that someone had recently—and mysteriously—died upstairs.

I had a hunch that Vera would ply us with freshly-baked goodies and hot drinks the moment we walked in. Sure enough, as soon as she opened the door, she asked,

"Would you like some banana bread? How about some tea or coffee?"

I grinned, never one to pass up banana bread. "Sure, I'll have a piece, and maybe some hot tea."

She scurried to the kitchen to prepare my food, and the doorbell rang. Waffles barked from the back yard, making it clear she was listening to our every move.

"Would you mind getting that?" Vera called.

I opened the door to Detective Hatcher. Although his brief smile managed to activate one of his dimples, it was clear from his serious gaze that he was here on business.

"Come in," I offered. "I just dropped in to be with Vera."

"Of course," he said. He knew we were close.

Vera hurried in, setting my tea and buttered bread slice on a side table, so I sat down in a chair next to it.

"Could I tempt you with some banana bread, or maybe tea or coffee, Charlie?" she asked.

Although Vera's use of his first name could have been disarming, the detective maintained his resolute look. "I'm afraid I don't have time for snacks today. Would you mind having a seat?"

Vera obediently sank into chair next to me, next to her own teacup.

The detective continued, "We've gotten the preliminary autopsy results. Goldie died of an illegal Fentanyl drug blend somewhere between eight and nine that night, and, given the traces on the glass shards in the bathroom, it seems to have been mixed into her eggnog. We know she drank eggnog, because her stomach contents included it, as well as chocolate and gingerbread, which I'm assuming came from cookies she'd eaten. As you can imagine, we'll need you to share as much as you can about serving the eggnog Friday night, Vera."

Her hand shook as she tried to pick up her teacup, and liquid splashed on her pants. She gave a yelp. "Oh, dear, that's hot."

The detective waited as she grabbed a tissue to dab at the wet spot. "Please, take your time."

She looked dismayed. "I really can't remember anything important. I served eggnog to nearly all my guests. The only one who doesn't like eggnog is Randall."

"Randall Mathena. Yes, he's on my list of attendees. Let me run it by you and see if I missed anyone."

As he read off each name, Vera nodded. When he reached the end, she said, "You didn't mention Doctor Schneider—I heard he came to pick Lena up. Did you see him, Macy?"

"I did. I went into the kitchen to get Lena for him. Let's see—I think he showed up just after Waffles got out."

The detective quirked an eyebrow. "You mean the dog escaped during the party? Didn't I see her crate there in the guest room?"

Vera managed to take a small sip of tea. "Yes, she was crated, then she somehow broke free and ran out among the guests. Macy got her." She shot me an appreciative look.

"You said you handed the mayor a glass of eggnog before she spoke. Did she set it down at any point? Did she drink it all during the meeting, or maybe get a refill?"

"I honestly wouldn't know," she said. "I left before the book discussion started to set foods out. Goldie could've helped herself to more eggnog and I wouldn't have noticed, since the punch bowl was at the opposite end of the island from where I was working."

He turned to me. "Did you notice Goldie's glass during book club?"

I tried to visualize where Goldie's eggnog glass had been located just before she picked up her hardcover book, but I was drawing a blank. I shook my head. "I don't remember, but maybe Rashana does. She was sitting on one side of her, and Randall on the other."

He seemed to take a different tack. "My officers dusted the open bathroom window for fingerprints and didn't find any. They also checked the roof for footprints, but the snow must've slid off earlier that night. Someone could've shimmied down that angled metal roof slope fairly easily, but any tracks below were covered by the pileup of roof snow. The open window likely melted the snow enough for it to slide off."

"Or someone knocked if off with them when they climbed down," Vera said.

"That's definitely possible." He crossed an ankle over his knee. "Vera, we found a bottle of what we call rainbow Fentanyl pills in the mayor's coat that was lying on your bed. It's a potent and illegal drug blend."

Vera looked horrified.

The detective continued. "We had the pills tested, and they seem to match what she was given—or what she took —before her death. She had a couple of pills' worth of Fentanyl in her system." He uncrossed his leg and leaned forward. "It doesn't sound like a lot, but I'll explain. Even one pill is far too heavy a dose. For example, open heart surgery patients might be given a half a milligram of Fentanyl. These home-blend pills can include up to two milligrams or more, which can easily kill someone, and Goldie's pills tested in at roughly a milligram and a half each." He took a deep breath. "Goldie had three milligrams in her, which basically stopped her breathing. Now, either she took a couple pills herself—and she should've known better, if those were her pills—or someone gave her a deliberate overdose."

I knew where he was going with this. "Are you treating this as a homicide, then?"

"We have to look at the possibility," he said. "We're not ruling out death by suicide, but it seems unlikely. Her husband said she loves her job, and he swears their relationship was stellar. I'll be looking into it, of course."

Vera nodded. "Goldie and Gary met later in life, and from all I could tell, they both felt they'd hit the jackpot." She shot an incredulous look at the detective. "I find it impossible to believe that Goldie was some kind of pill-head. She was always alert and prepared—that's why I chose her to lead our book discussions."

He seemed sympathetic. "I understand. We're examining every option, but I wanted to keep you posted as to the direction of our inquiries."

"Thank you," Vera said quietly.

The detective stood. "I'd better get back, but if anything relevant comes to mind, please let me know immediately."

"We will," I said, standing to walk him to the door. Vera remained seated, apparently lost in thought.

As the detective stepped onto the porch, I whispered, "This whole thing is a shock for her."

"I know, and I'm sorry she's been put in this position, believe me." He dipped his head before clomping down the stairs in his sturdy boots. Obviously, he couldn't say

anything more to ease my mind, at least until circum-
stances surrounding Goldie's death were clearer. But, at
the same time, I wished he could reassure me that Vera
wasn't ever going to be a serious suspect in Goldie's death,
even though she'd been the one to serve Goldie eggnog—
in front of the entire book club.

LATER IN THE AFTERNOON, Dylan dropped into the cafe. He
picked up a couple of to-go drinks, and I figured one of
them was for his gallery assistant, Shanda. He was the kind
of humble boss who brought his assistant coffee, instead of
the other way around.

With cups in hand, he walked over to the Barks section
and stood outside the gate. After taking a sip of his brew,
he greeted me and said, "I wanted to let you know there's a
watercolor class at the gallery tonight. Since you've been
looking into people who were at the book club party, I
thought you might want to drop in. Nancy Gill will be
attending."

I tried to look innocent. Placing a hand to my heart, I
said, "Who, me, looking into things?"

Even behind the artsy dark glasses he wore to work, I
could tell Dylan's smile reached his eyes. "I know you fairly
well, Macy. There's no way you can resist getting involved
so you can bring Vera some peace of mind. I just thought
I'd help you out."

I grinned. "Thanks for thinking of me. Maybe I will
show up."

He set the other coffee on the divider wall, but picked it
up the moment Copper started sniffing at it. "It should be

an interesting night. To keep your cover, you'll want to paint something, but your art supplies will be on the house, and I'll cover your class fee."

I froze. "I'm no good at artwork. I can't even draw a decent dog."

"Just do something non-representational. Paint a mood versus a scene, that kind of thing. I'll stop by and help, if you need it."

"Oh, believe me, I'll need it." I stepped aside as a mom and two teen boys walked into the Barks section. Copper immediately perked up, making her way toward the teens. "I'd better get back to my job. Enjoy your coffee, and please tell Shanda I said hello."

"Will do. I think you'll have a good time tonight. If nothing else, our finger foods will be catered from that fusion restaurant my friend owns."

It was a place we'd once gone on a date, and he probably remembered how much I'd liked the meal. "I'll look forward to that. Thanks, Dylan."

I turned back to the mother and her sons. After making a little conversation, I learned she was a home-schooler who had brought her boys over to show them an example of a successful start-up business. Flattered at her high level of respect, I told her they should go over and talk with Bo, who was the real mastermind behind the Barks & Beans Cafe.

But her boys were already preoccupied with Copper, who seemed to have taken a serious shine to them. The ginger dog wove between their legs, acting more frisky than I'd ever seen her. Summer had stressed that Copper needed someone to keep her active, and I sensed this might be a match made in heaven.

"I'll ask my brother to come over and speak with you all," I offered. I could fill in for Bo while he chatted in the Barks section.

Once we'd switched places, I mentioned the watercolor class to Bristol.

"Would you want to join me?" I asked, knowing she could walk into a class like that and blow everyone away with her artistic talent.

"I have a date tonight," she said. Her creamy white cheeks colored a little. "It's actually with Milo."

"Aw! You two are dating now?" We'd all known it was inevitable, given the natural friendship they shared.

She nodded. "He's taking me to his brother's house for some kind of poker club—The Barons, I think they're called. Sounds utterly pretentious, but at least I can get to know his family a little."

"I'm sure you'll have a nice time." Milo's brother Hudson was the kind of guy who'd never met a stranger, so I was sure he'd be welcoming. I'd visited The Barons myself just recently, when I was trying to get a closer look at the elite circles in town.

"Well, I don't plan to gamble," she added. "I need all my funds for college."

I gave her a hug. "I know your mom would be glad to hear that."

Bo returned to the coffee bar. "Your turn," he said. "I'm pretty sure those guys have fallen for that overweight dog."

While my brother certainly hadn't minced words, I knew he was just as happy about a possible dog adoption as I was. "I'm on it," I said, walking over to encourage the mom to stop by the shelter and fill out paperwork so Copper could join their family soon.

9

Bo dropped in to give me some fried chicken and fresh pasta salad before I headed over to The Discerning Palette for my watercolor class. "Way to go, getting that cute dog adopted today," he said.

Coal sat down and pressed his head against Bo's leg, closing his eyes as if my brother were his favorite person in the world. In reality, my Great Dane had plenty of admirers he could hit up for a little extra attention when they came to visit.

Bo obligingly rubbed behind Coal's upright ears, so I caught him up on Detective Hatcher's chat with Vera. I explained that I was heading to the painting class in hopes of talking with Nancy Gill.

He cringed. "According to Cully, Emory won't stop pestering him to give him the mayor position. If the police are entertaining the idea that Goldie might've been murdered, I want you to be careful tonight. You never know how desperate the Gills were for him to get that job."

"I'll be careful. Anyway, Dylan's there."

Bo gave me a raised-eyebrow look.

I was instantly defensive. "What? Dylan knows we're just friends, if that's what you're wondering about."

"Of course, sis. I'm not questioning your loyalty to Titan. And I know you'd never let Dylan get the wrong impression about things. But I'm a dude, and I know how dudes think, and I'm just saying maybe you shouldn't hang out quite so much with Dylan."

"You're just overreacting because Tara broke your engagement when she believed the lies someone told about you." I stopped short when I saw Bo's hurt look. "I'm sorry."

"It's okay. I know how it must've sounded to Tara when I told her the lady at work had cooked up that story that I was seeing her on the side. But that's the rub—there's no defensible position when someone paints you out to be the bad guy. I know Dylan would never do that to you, but there are gossips like Matilda around."

I gave him a hug. "I'll explain things to Titan. I'm sure he'll understand, because we've discussed my friendship with Dylan in the past." I frowned. "I just wish we knew why that woman lied about you at Coffee Mass. She was determined to break up your engagement."

"I'm fairly certain Leo Moreau set that up. He wanted my personal life to get so distracting that I had to stop tracking all his illegal operations. And when you think about it, his tactic worked. I had to retire early and move across the country. My engagement was shot." He shook his head.

Leo Moreau was a crime lord who had wreaked all kinds of havoc, from drug trade to human trafficking, even here in West Virginia. But just this year, Leo's wife had given Bo a tip, allowing him to track down a witness in Ecuador who was willing to testify about Leo's illegal trade in South America.

As a result, Leo was now safely behind bars, but Titan, Bo, and I suspected that his wife, Anne Louise, might have covertly taken the reins to her husband's crime empire. The FBI hadn't been able to prove anything yet, but she was shockingly well-connected, even in Lewisburg.

I tried to cheer Bo up. "Well, Leo's plan actually worked out for good, so on some level, I guess we owe him a huge thanks. After all, Summer is a far better woman than Tara ever was. I'm still convinced Tara was a raging narcissist. She never cared about anyone but herself."

This brought a smile to his face. "You're always saying how I'm the protective sibling, but I have the feeling you would've given Tara quite the comeuppance, given half the chance."

"You're right. Love ya, bro."

"Love you, too. Have a good night, and let me know if you pick up any good painting tips—or any helpful information on Nancy and Emory Gill."

THE DISCERNING PALETTE was hopping by the time I arrived, which was five minutes after class signups had opened. Unlike my brother, I preferred not to arrive everywhere fifteen minutes ahead of time to get the "lay of the land," as he called it.

The line appeared to be dwindling, but Shanda hurried my way and pulled me out of it. "I hope you don't mind, but I took the liberty of signing you up since Dylan said you'd be coming tonight. I've set up your supplies over here." She led me toward a long table where paper, water, and paints had been placed at each seat. Motioning toward a chair near the end of the table, she said, "This spot's yours."

I sat down before glancing around. Nancy Gill was already seated three chairs from me, and she gave me a cursory nod. "Hello, Macy." Her dismissive tone made it clear she wasn't pleased to see me.

I responded with a polite hello, then felt someone walk up behind me. Assuming it was Dylan, I turned, then my smile quickly disappeared. Emory Gill stood with his hands on his hips, his tiny eyes shooting daggers my way.

"Why, if it isn't Macy Hatfield. I'm surprised you're out and about like this, since your cafe is so exclusive."

I couldn't believe those words actually came out of his mouth. Before I could formulate a response, Dylan strode over and clamped a firm hand on Emory's shoulder. His long fingers curled, as if locking the rude man in place.

"Mr. Gill. Were you signed up for the class tonight? We'll be starting in a few moments."

Emory made a sputtering noise. "Well, no. I was just here to drop my wife off. Though she hardly needs a class. As you know, she's an artist in her own right—"

"Of course," Dylan interrupted. "But we'll need to leave this section so our attendees can focus. I'm sure you understand." His tone said, "You'd *better* understand and come with me."

Emory said, "Goodbye, my dear," to Nancy, who gave him a halfhearted wave. Maybe she could only tolerate her husband up to a point.

Shanda carried some finger foods and small plates

over, setting them in the middle of the table. "Feel free to pick at these as you paint," she said. As she walked by me, she whispered, "Dylan ordered extra pork hand rolls for you since he knew they're your favorite."

I smiled, grabbing a plate and helping myself to a couple of rolls. A woman I assumed was the teacher walked in and stood at the head of the table.

I'd just taken a bite when Cully Stone entered the room. Nancy gave him a piercing stare before getting distracted by the teacher, who was setting up one of her paintings for us to look at.

Cully walked right over and sat down at the empty place beside me. He gave me a genuine smile. His light brown hair was fading to gray, and he wore a sweater vest that reminded me of a kindly uncle.

The teacher introduced herself as Mrs. Hamrick and began to explain how watercolor painting worked. Once she'd finally left us to our own devices, Cully leaned in and said, "How's your brother? I know you and he are close, just like my daughters are with each other. They live in different states, but they call each other about every day." He fiddled with his brush. "Do you think Bo's considering what I asked him about?"

Of course, I knew exactly what he was referring to, but it wouldn't be wise to mention the mayor position with Nancy sitting so close by. She was already shooting curious looks our way.

I took another bite of pork roll in an attempt to stall any actual painting I'd have to do. "I think he is, yes."

"Good." Cully brushed light yellow paint across the paper, mimicking the washing technique Mrs. Hamrick had shown us.

Sighing, I tried to mix a light pink shade for my wash. "But what about Rashana?" I whispered. "I understood she wanted to be mayor."

Cully gave a vigorous shake of his head, nearly flipping his brush off the paper. "She let us down in a big way with a public safety project this year. I won't go into details, but suffice it to say, I'd feel much better knowing Bo was in charge of that aspect of things. He has experience in these matters, and he's friends with Charlie Hatcher, so they could work together well. I could even shuffle a bit more power to him in that arena, since my plate is full enough."

"That does sound like a good fit," I said. The job almost seemed tailor-made for my brother.

As Cully returned to his painting, I tried to look at my pink-washed paper objectively. It seemed to need a little something—maybe grass—to anchor the bottom. After squeezing green paint onto my disposable palette, I dipped my brush into it, then swept it across the paper. What I wound up with was a rather horrifying shade of electric chartreuse that I would need to cover with a darker green. As I scrambled to rectify my mistake, Dylan walked past and made a noise that sounded suspiciously like a repressed laugh.

About halfway through, Mrs. Hamrick suggested we take a short break. I stood and stretched, visiting the drink table to pour myself a mug of chamomile tea.

Nancy skulked up behind me. She didn't seem anxious to converse, but I turned to talk to her anyway. After all, she was the reason I'd come.

"I feel like I'm learning a lot," I said.

She shrugged. "It's very basic, but I suppose it's helpful if you're just starting out."

Hoping to ask Nancy a few pointed questions, I stepped out of her way, then gently steered the conversation toward what I wanted to discuss. "I really enjoyed my book club visit," I said. "Vera's food is always top-notch."

To my surprise, Nancy's face softened. She poured herself a cup of decaf coffee. "Poor Vera. I hate that her party turned out so badly in the end. Her eggnog is always a highlight of the year. She actually gave me her recipe, so I'm planning to put a little peppermint twist on it when my children come to visit this Christmas." She actually seemed at ease talking about her plans for the holidays.

Hoping to keep the goodwill going, I continued. "Vera was so excited about the party. I helped her put up a bunch of decorations—did you see that silver tree she had upstairs?" It was a trick question, because that particular tree was only visible if you walked all the way up the stairs and stepped onto the landing.

But Nancy didn't take the bait. Stirring a creamer packet into her decaf coffee, she said, "I didn't. I headed home as soon as I heard I didn't win a gift basket." She gave me a disappointed look. "I wonder what happened to Goldie's basket. I suppose Rashana kept it. It's a shame, because I was really hoping to try some of your coffee. "

I didn't see how winning a gift basket was her only chance to sample Barks & Beans coffee, but maybe her husband's bad behavior at the cafe had made her feel hesitant to visit. "I'm sorry," I said. "If you come by the cafe, you can ask for a free house blend on me."

After flashing a brief smile of appreciation, her look hardened. "Thanks, but Emory said he's not welcome there, so I probably won't drop in."

I took a deep breath. "Emory was publicly belittling the

mayor, who had just died. So yes, he was asked to leave. But *you* are welcome to drop in anytime."

Dylan walked up. "Did you try the pork hand rolls?" he asked.

Knowing he was worried I was about to get into it with Nancy, I said, "Yes. I think I'll get one more before we start."

ONCE I'D PUT the finishing touches on my painting, I actually felt pleased with it. I'd followed Dylan's advice to stick with an abstract kind of vibe, which wound up looking like a flower garden with pale gray clouds floating overhead. Even though one of the puffiest clouds undeniably resembled Coal's head, I was considering framing my first venture into watercolors.

Nancy had already gone home as I started to gather up my things. I said goodbye to Cully, who was nibbling on a mini eggroll as he finished his painting.

"Please tell Bo I could really use him," he said. "And honestly, the sooner, the better."

"I'll tell him." Tucking my painting into the folder they had provided, I headed toward the front of the gallery.

Before I could open the door, Dylan left off his conversation with Mrs. Hamrick and jogged over to catch me. "How did it go? Did you learn anything helpful?"

"Not really. It sounds like Nancy never went upstairs that night."

He clicked his tongue. "Her husband Emory is a real piece of work, though. I didn't like how he was talking to you. I can only imagine that your brother wouldn't, either."

"They've already clashed, which was probably the

reason Emory was attacking me." I pulled my gloves from my pocket and slipped them on. As I pushed the door open, a gust of chilly air rushed in.

"It must be twenty degrees out there," Dylan observed. "Could I give you a ride home?"

I let the door close and thought about it a moment. Bo's admonition popped into my head, but I dismissed it. I shouldn't feel guilty for having a friend drive me the short distance home because I didn't really want to walk against the bitter wind.

"Sure."

Once he'd told Shanda he'd be right back, Dylan led me out to his car in the gallery parking lot. It only took about five minutes to get home, and we sat in companionable silence the entire way, waiting for the heat to kick on. Predictably, it finally did the moment he pulled up to the curb outside my house.

"Nice try on the heat." I laughed.

"Sorry." He turned toward me, and light from the street lamp reflected off his glasses. I could sense he wanted to say something. He cleared his throat. "So you're happy with Titan, right?"

"What? Why would you ask that? Of course I am." I hoped this conversation wasn't going the way it seemed to be going.

"It's just that you're so fun to hang out with. We talk art together, play video games together...I don't know. It's like you've gotten into my head, and I can't seem to get you out, no matter how hard I try." He rested his arm next to mine on the console. "And I have been trying, Macy, I swear."

I gave his hand a platonic pat. "I understand what you're saying, but Dylan, we have fun together because we're *friends*. I'm not right for you romantically. I thought we'd already hashed this out."

He offered a slow smile, his white teeth gleaming in the near-dark. "I believe *you* were the one doing all the hashing. I just had to go along with your evaluation of our relationship, as I recall."

I sighed. "Well, feel free to throw some hash my way, but it won't change the fact that I'm taken." I hated to be cold, but Dylan had to get it through his head that I wasn't interested in him. Vera's suggestion of finding someone to set him up with was sounding better and better.

"Okay, I understand. I just needed to make sure you were in a good situation with him, and it sounds like it." He said *him* as if he couldn't bring himself to articulate Titan's name. Turning to face the windshield, he placed a hand on the wheel, like he was ready to roll on out of this awkwardness.

"Thanks for being honest with me." I gave his shoulder a brief pat before opening my door. "And thanks for the ride."

"Happy to help." He leaned forward to add, "By the way, this doesn't change anything. We're still friends. If you need any more help looking into Goldie's death, I'm here for you."

10

After letting Coal out for his nightly constitutional, I called Summer to talk about what had just happened with Dylan. I wasn't even sure how to feel about it at this stage.

She listened in silence as I shared. When I finally got quiet, she said, "You did the right thing. You let him know it wasn't going anywhere, but it doesn't sound like you were too harsh about it at all."

As usual, Summer got to the heart of what I wasn't even aware I was worrying about. "Thanks. That does help. You should've been a psychologist," I joked.

"Speaking of which, did you ever follow up with Doctor Schneider? You said he'd helped you that one time you talked with him. I thought you were going to try to set up an appointment with him."

Coal bumped his nose into the screen door, so I walked over to let him in. Snow had gotten trapped in his paws, so as he walked, icy chunks dropped off onto the wood floors. I put the phone on speaker, grabbed a kitchen towel, and tried to wipe his paws down. "Good suggestion. I was just thinking of seeing him again." I didn't add that my main motivation—as with my last visit—was to check into the psychologist's alibi.

SINCE TUESDAY WAS my day off, I gave in to my lazier inclinations and slept late. When I finally woke, I felt refreshed and ready to tackle the task I'd set for myself—visiting Doctor Schneider at Ivy Hill. I'd called and asked when would be a good time to drop by, and he'd said right around 12:30 on his lunch break.

Long ago, I'd learned by watching Auntie A that you don't approach people for favors without bringing something along with you to grease the gears. I couldn't count the number of times she'd lifted some of her prize iris bulbs to take to friends, or packed up a jar of her apple butter or peach jam to offer when we dropped in.

Since I didn't attempt canning and it certainly wasn't the time of year to plant bulbs, I decided to take one of my bags of leftover house blend coffee to the psychologist. Hopefully my gift would warm him up, so he'd be ready to answer a few questions about book club night.

For instance, he had come by early to pick up Lena—right after Waffles had gotten loose. Was that a coincidence? Both Vera and Randall couldn't fathom how the dog's crate could've opened without human intervention, so it was possible someone might've wanted a distraction from Goldie's drama in the bathroom upstairs. While I was certain the doctor wouldn't have been able to slip down the hallway unnoticed, maybe he'd seen someone creeping around outside.

I also wanted to give him a gentle heads-up that people were talking about his visit to Goldie's house. I knew he wouldn't take offense, and it seemed best to give him the chance to explain things to his wife, who was clearly concerned about his loyalty.

I hadn't been to Ivy Hill for many months. It was always a bittersweet experience to drive along the sweeping golf course, because Coal's first owner had been murdered on the grounds. Gerard had been a golf instructor, and not someone of the highest character, it had turned out. I hated that he had been so brutally murdered, but at the same time, if Doctor Schneider hadn't taken Gerard's ownerless Great Dane to the shelter, I never would've had the chance to adopt one of the best dogs on earth.

The center itself, a sprawling Tudor house that had been expanded on both ends, still looked much the same. It dominated the top of a barren hill, although I was happy to see they'd planted some trees since the last time I'd visited. A fountain—now covered for winter—sat in the middle of a circular drive paved with terracotta bricks.

After parking, I knocked on the large oak door. A tall, tanned blonde opened it. She took one look at me before throwing her arms around my neck. "Macy! Girl, you haven't been by in forever. Were you having a look around before bringing the shelter dogs in January? Our residents are already so excited about meeting them."

Katie Givens and I had formed an unlikely friendship on the other end of Gerard's death. I knew she had a heart for the men and women who enrolled in the rehab program at the center, and she had the kind of dauntless energy it took to make a business succeed.

I smiled. "Not this time, I'm afraid. I came to ask Doctor Schneider a quick question."

She looked disappointed. "I would've loved to chat with you over a cup of tea from our new cafe. Granted, we only carry health foods, so it would be herbal, but I'm sure you'd like the pomegranate raspberry blend."

"Sounds tasty. I promise I'll drop in before we bring the dogs, so we can have a proper visit."

Thus appeased, Katie gave me another hug, then headed down the hallway, presumably to her office. As always, the entryway was entirely lit with battery-operated candles and twinkle lights, which made it seem like a cozy cave. I headed up the carpeted stairs to Doctor Schneider's door and gave it a knock.

"Come right on in," he said.

The doctor's office hadn't changed much since the last time I'd seen it. I took a deep breath of the earthy scent that permeated the room, thanks in large part to the plants crowded along the walls and windowsills. An indoor waterfall feature gurgled in the background, making me feel like I'd stepped into a peaceful rainforest.

He gestured to the worn velvet chair I'd sat in when I had shared with him about my parents' deaths. It had started as a cover story, my opening up to him for a free therapy session, but it had ended up with me realizing I had buried my grief so deep I didn't even know how to process any of it. Now that I was seated opposite the good-natured man once again, I felt the urge to spill everything, but I knew I had to stay on topic.

"What can I do for you today, Miss Hatfield?" he asked. "You said you had something to talk with me about."

"First, I'd like you to have this." I placed the bag of coffee on his desk. "I know Lena already won some in her book club basket, but a little extra coffee never hurts."

He gave me a wide smile. "That's for sure. There's no coffee in our cafe downstairs, so I fill my travel mug with java every morning. I'm far from the health purist Katie is. I'll enjoy drinking it." He placed his elbows on his paper-strewn desk, and I had to grin because his red pullover sweater seemed an unwitting homage to his Santa Claus appearance. "Now, how can I help you?"

"Doctor Schneider, you came early to pick up Lena from the book club party. I wondered if you happened to see anyone lurking around outside Vera's house?" If he had, maybe he hadn't understood the significance of it.

He lowered his bushy white brows. "The snow was coming down thick, so I might not have noticed if someone was. But no, I don't recall seeing anybody out there."

"Okay. Thanks for that information." I sank back into the chair, which seemed to mold to my body, almost hugging it. "I love this chair," I remarked.

"Isn't it wonderful? I got it years ago at a quirky antique store outside Charleston, South Carolina. It cost me thirty dollars." He chuckled.

I let out a slow breath, trying to brace myself for the next topic. "I have something I need to ask you about, but it's a bit unpleasant."

He turned serious. "I assure you, it takes a lot to surprise me. In fact, sometimes I wonder if anyone can anymore. I think I've heard it all. I feel bad for Lena, having to put up with such a jaded old coot."

"You and Lena seem very close. But I have to ask if there was any sort of...personal interest between you and Goldie Keaton?"

He frowned. "No, there wasn't. Whatever gave you that impression?"

It was time to place my cards on the table. "Matilda Crump has a friend in Goldie's neighborhood, and she saw you coming out of the mayor's house one night."

With a short, bitter laugh, the psychologist said, "So *that's* why all those women were shooting me dirty looks when I picked Lena up. Matilda Crump was spying on me —I should've known. I've always been baffled as to why Lena decided to befriend that woman when she returned to Lewisburg."

He was quite gruff, but he really had every right to be. Matilda had basically been slandering him across town.

He folded his hands, resting them on the desk. "To answer your question, no, Goldie and I weren't having some kind of affair. The night Matilda's friend spotted me, I was dropping off a book—a counseling book I'd recommended in my office earlier that day, to be specific." He gave me a pointed look, and I realized what he was insinuating.

"You were counseling her," I said quietly. "Was she having some kind of emotional problems that might lead to her trying to harm herself, would you say?"

His expression was neutral. "I really can't say anything else. Doctor-patient confidentiality and all that."

"I understand." I tried to give him a winning smile. "Doctor, I appreciate your time. I don't want to barge into your personal life, but I would strongly recommend you tell your wife that Goldie was only a patient and that you were dropping off a counseling book that night. I think she's already heard about it secondhand."

"With a friend like Matilda, I wouldn't be surprised," he said. "Thank you for your thoughtfulness. I know you're looking out for my best interests, as well as Lena's. I'll talk with her."

As I reluctantly evacuated the coziest chair I'd ever sat in, Doctor Schneider asked, "How are you *actually* doing, Macy? I know you keep busy at the cafe and you love working with dogs. But I mean how are you doing personally?"

Something about the psychologist's deep, easy tone always poked holes in my dammed-up emotions. I brushed away a rogue tear that dropped to my cheek. How was I *really* doing? I hardly ever took the time to think about it. I tried to keep moving forward, because looking back was far too painful.

I didn't quite feel the cheer I had to force into my words. "I'm great."

After all, wasn't I doing great? I had a thoughtful, loving boyfriend, a loyal canine companion, a sweet next-door neighbor, and a brother who would lay down his life for me. Didn't I have it all?

Doctor Schneider nodded. "Okay. But if you ever want to talk about anything, just call. We'll fit you in."

Just as I'd done the last time I'd visited his office, I assured him I'd be in touch. But deep down, I knew I wasn't ready to explore the losses I'd experienced in life, and I might not ever be.

11

Back home, I used the leftover fried chicken and a slice of cheddar to throw together a quick sandwich. I added some of my remaining pasta salad on the side. I'd just about finished my lunch when Summer called.

"Hey, today's my day off, and Bo told me it's yours, too," she said. "Want to do something together? I'm just sitting at home, petting my cats."

I laughed. "Crazy cat lady, eh?"

Coal shot me a look from his pillow, as if he fully understood the meaning of the word "cat." He probably thought he was going to visit Stormy soon.

"Let me think." I took my last bite of pasta salad and considered our options. "I have a good idea. Would you want to take a walk along the river trail?" Although it was still chilly, it had warmed up considerably since last night, and I felt the driving need to burn off some energy.

Summer sounded excited. "That sounds great. Usually, the extent of my exercise routine is wrangling pets into kennels. A long walk along the river with my bestie sounds so much better."

Quietly flattered to be called Summer's "bestie," I said, "Great. I'll pick you up in about twenty minutes. Is it okay if I bring Coal?"

"Always. You know I love that big sweetie."

WHEN I PULLED out Coal's plaid fleece-lined harness, he seemed willing enough to wear it, since that meant he'd be taking a longer walk with me. But it took me a while to recall which way the harness went, and once I'd figured that out, Coal kept nervously sitting down. It took forever to maneuver the fleece over his enormous torso.

I was about ten minutes late when I pulled up to Summer's place. She jogged out, sporting loose gray sweatpants that fit like they were made in the nineties, along with a violet ear warmer headband and matching gloves. Although she might not be the height of fashion today, she was definitely ready for the cold.

"Did you get held up?" she asked.

I glanced at Coal, who was sitting with his front paws demurely crossed on my fold-out back seat. He gave me a superior look, as if I were his minion and he'd had nothing to do with our tardiness.

"Uh, yeah—sorry. It took me a little while to get him into that fleece, but he'll be glad I did," I said.

On the way over, Summer asked how things were going with Vera, so I caught her up on my suspicions. "I've looked into Nancy's story, as well as Doctor Schneider's. Neither of them seems to be involved in Goldie's murder."

"*If* she was even murdered in the first place," Summer mused. "It could've just been a massive drug overdose. Those things happen so fast." The way she said it hinted that she'd seen someone overdose, but she didn't make any effort to enlighten me as to who that might have been. Summer definitely had her secrets—especially when it came to the Mennonite family she'd walked away from.

"Right." I pulled into a parking lot near the trail, then turned to put Coal's soft muzzle on. "It's a necessary evil, my boy. We'll be walking near a lot of people who'll be terrified of your size."

"You're doing the right thing," Summer said. "Even trustworthy dogs can get skittish around strangers—and strange dogs."

As we walked onto the wooded trail, Summer said, "I've been wondering about Tara. Bo doesn't ever mention her, but I'm curious as to what she was *like*, you know?"

"Nothing like you, I can tell you that," I said. "Back when Bo met her in California, he fell pretty hard." I wasn't trying to hurt Summer, but I needed to point out the contrast in relationships so she could see that Bo truly loved her more. "They did sporty things together, like surfing and rock-climbing. Bo cooked for her, got her car inspected, watered her yard—you name it. He was kind of like a puppy, at her beck and call."

Summer broke into a power stride, so I had to take more steps to keep up. My short legs didn't cover as much ground as her longer ones. "That's interesting. He's not like that with me," she said.

I grabbed her arm so she'd have to meet my eyes. In front of us, Coal slowed in response to my pressure on his leash.

"But that's the point," I said. "Bo wasn't truly himself with her. She was driven, but we both know Bo is, too. They were like fire and gasoline. It never could've worked in the long run, even though there were plenty of sparks at first. He needed someone completely different—someone less aggressive. Someone who's truly thoughtful of others and who would never dream of taking advantage of his boundless affection. Someone he could love for a lifetime." I stopped short, realizing I was on the brink of letting on that she'd soon get a proposal.

To my relief, her walk slowed. "You're the best, Macy. I've thought this through so many times, but I've never connected the dots in that way. I know you're always saying I'm the instinctual one, but when it comes to Bo, I'm completely blinded by love. Back before we started dating, I'd noticed those pictures of Tara in his kitchen, and she looked so glamorous, so self-assured. I'm nothing like that."

"She was fake, and I didn't like her," I said. "So there's no way it could've worked."

Summer grinned and took a deep breath. "I'm so glad we're friends," she said.

"Of course we are, bestie."

We walked in silence, the quiet green river rippling along the right side of the trail. "It's flowing pretty steady today," Summer observed. She glanced behind us. "You know, we've hardly seen anyone out here. People must've assumed it would be too cold, but it's really not bad when you get the blood pumping."

I only hoped Summer didn't plan on pumping her speedy legs again.

As we came to an opening in the trees that led to the

flat river rocks below, Coal stopped short. He sniffed at the
air, then made some kind of growling grunt inside his
muzzle.

Summer pointed to the riverbank. "What's that?"

Something big and sapphire blue bobbed along the
water's edge. It took me a moment to realize what we were
looking at. "It's someone's jacket," I said. "Must've gotten
stuck on a branch."

Coal was becoming increasingly agitated. He pulled at
his leash, nearly yanking me off my feet. "Hey, watch it!" I
scolded.

Summer was already making her way down the rock
stairs toward the open area. "We should at least check it
out," she said.

I rolled my eyes, knowing it would take Coal some time
to pick his way down the incline of the muddy stairs.
"Thanks a lot, buddy," I grumbled under my breath.

By the time we reached the flat rocks below, Summer
was nearly at the river's edge. Coal gave another jerk at his
leash, so I let him go, unwilling to get dragged behind him.

"Oh, good heavens!" Summer grabbed Coal's collar and
pulled him up short before he could sniff at the jacket.
"Macy, get over here!"

I headed her way. As I neared the edge, I realized what
I'd assumed was a jacket was actually a soggy hoodie.

And around the sides of the pulled-up hood, curly
black hair floated on the surface.

"Oh, no," I breathed, realizing we were looking at a
woman, lying face-down in the water.

Without a word, Summer handed Coal off to me, then
fished her hand into the river to retrieve the woman's wrist.
Water dripped from the woman's lifeless fingers as

Summer checked for a pulse. "She's dead. I'm going to turn her over. Just keep your grip on snoop doggie there."

My fingers tightened around Coal's leather collar. What a good dog he'd been to point out this woman's body to us. He sat down close to my feet, probably sensing I was rattled.

As Summer tried to roll the waterlogged body over, it became obvious that the woman's sleeve had snagged on a protruding branch. After carefully extricating the sleeve, Summer first eased the body onto its side, then onto its back.

I jolted to recognize Rashana's brown eyes, once so bright, now staring blankly at the sky. Her face had turned an unnaturally ashy shade and her lips looked puffy. The front of her bright blue hoodie was emblazoned with an oversized Reebok logo, but it had been marred by an ugly dark smudge in the middle.

Summer pointed to the discolored area. "That doesn't look right. I'm going to get her out of the water." With a few forceful tugs, she managed to drag the upper portion of Rashana's body onto a rock. She glanced toward the trail, but so far, no one had noticed what we were doing.

"Do you think that's blood?" I darted a glance toward the dark spot. My stomach lurched, giving me a warning to look away. More than once in my life, the sight of blood had brought me to the brink of passing out. Coal backed up and pressed against my leg, as if he sensed I could fall over at any moment. "I'd better call Charlie," I suggested.

"Yes, you should." She was leaning over the body. "If you look close, you can see the fabric's been sliced in the middle of that stain."

I had no wish to look closely at anything, so I fumbled for my phone.

But Summer had already grabbed a twig and was gently lifting the lower part of the hoodie, revealing the bottom edge of Rashana's gray tank top. I averted my eyes before the middle of the tank was exposed.

Summer gasped. "Someone's definitely stabbed her, see? There's more blood here, around a big cut."

Summer wasn't aware that I was so sensitive to blood, but just her mention of the stab wound was making me feel woozy. I jabbed urgently at Charlie's contact number on my phone screen, hoping I could share what had happened without keeling over.

Finally, just when I was about to go to voicemail, the detective picked up. "Sorry I didn't answer sooner—I had to find my phone. I'd left it in my coat pocket. What's going on?"

I sank onto a nearby rock and told him everything, then assured him we'd stay with Rashana until he and his officers arrived. "We're right past the outhouse, at the wider rocky area by the river," I explained. "We've gotten her out of the water."

Another detective might have made some kind of crack about how I'd been first on the scene in both Goldie's and now Rashana's deaths, but Charlie didn't even attempt it. He requested that we keep people away from the body, but that was about the size of it.

When I reported back to Summer, she gestured toward the bottom of the stairs. "Maybe you should take Coal and stand over there, so you can tell people they can't come down. They wouldn't dare try to get past him." She glanced at Rashana. "I'm going to try to drag her a bit farther back so her shoes can drain out some."

"Good idea," I said, happy to put some distance between me and Rashana's body. Coal and I walked toward the stairs, where a twenty-something couple was peering over the bank.

"Please stay there," I said. "Don't come down. Police are on their way."

The young woman held up her phone and pointed it at Rashana. "Is that a dead person?"

Although I understood that reaching for a phone was the first instinct of her generation, I said, "Please don't take any photos or video."

She huffed, "It doesn't matter much now, does it?"

Coal gave a low rumble in response to her challenging tone, and the man's face blanched. "Come on, Mazzy. Let's get going, like the nice lady said."

They walked away, but they were soon replaced with more bystanders. By the time the paramedics, police officers, and Detective Hatcher arrived, quite a crowd had gathered. Police tape was quickly strung and onlookers cleared away. After examining the scene, the detective came over to the log where Summer and I had sat down with Coal.

"I take it you didn't find a phone on her?" he asked.

Summer shook her head. "I didn't go through her pockets."

"We did, and we couldn't find one." He threw a glance toward Rashana's covered body. "I'm going to get in a request to tap her location services—maybe we'll locate her phone that way. You ladies—and Coal—can get on home. Thanks for all you've done."

Coal gave a friendly thump of his tail. He'd met the detective before and liked him.

"Please let us know if you find anything," I said. "I don't know if she had any significant other or family around, but she worked at The Greenbrier."

He nodded. "I was aware of that. Her parents moved into the Alderson area just last year—I met them at a strawberry festival. I'm getting their address now, so I can tell them before we release this to the news." He turned and headed back toward his officers.

Summer stood, and Coal jumped to his feet, anxious to get moving. I clicked his muzzle back into place, since I'd taken it off while we were sitting. I helped him up the rock stairs and back onto the trail, where Summer seemed to breathe a sigh of relief.

"I'll never look at this trail the same way again," she said. "I wonder if Rashana was stabbed along the trail and dumped into the river, or if she was stabbed elsewhere and then dropped off."

"It can't be a coincidence that she was found on the same trail where Goldie was seen talking with a drug courier. I need to let Bo know about this, and probably Titan, too."

"Definitely."

When we got back to the car, I gave Bo a call. He said he'd ask the detective to keep him in the loop, and he'd let Cully know what had happened.

I called Titan next, but he seemed perturbed about Rashana's stabbing. "You're telling me that the mayor and a city council member died within the space of a week—and one was clearly murdered? Plus, drugs were definitely involved in the mayor's death?"

It sounded even worse when he put it that way. "That's right."

Coal heaved a huge sigh. He was already lying down in the back, preparing to conk out from his strenuous afternoon. Summer was guzzling water as if she'd run a marathon in the blazing heat.

"I'd advise Bo not to become mayor until these deaths are squared away," Titan continued.

"You might have to do that kind of advising," I said. "The city manager seems anxious to fill the position, and you know Bo doesn't relish a vacuum of authority."

"True. He'll feel the need to step in." Titan paused. "I'll give him a call tonight. And Macy, please be careful yourself. I don't like the sound of what's going on around there."

I could tell that was an understatement. For a man who regularly faced life-threatening situations to say something unsavory was going on in town was roughly equivalent to Paul Revere warning that the British were coming.

"I will," I said.

As I pulled out of the parking lot, I tried to imagine who could stab someone as friendly as Rashana in cold blood. The woman planned weddings, for goodness' sake.

Titan was right. Whatever was going on in my hometown was dark, and I had the unsettling feeling it wasn't over yet.

12

The temperatures had plunged into the high teens by Wednesday morning, so I pulled on the knit socks Titan's mother had sent me at Thanksgiving. She'd found the softest wool in my favorite colors to make a pair of socks that I would treasure. It was one of the sweetest things anyone had ever done for me.

At the cafe, Milo and Bristol were joking around as they prepped the machines. Unwilling to disturb them, I headed for the Barks section and straightened up until Summer brought the dogs in. She looked like she hadn't slept well.

"I couldn't stop thinking about that stab wound," she said, her voice lowered. "It wasn't like what you see on TV."

"These things rarely are." I sounded like some kind of world-weary traveler who'd seen it all.

"I don't think it was a crime of passion," she mused. "She was only stabbed the one time, and it was such a clean cut, you know? Like someone wanted to get it over with."

Summer was onto something there. While stabbings were violent crimes, Rashana's stabbing somehow seemed...quieter. More half-hearted, like the killer didn't even care to make sure she was dead.

I'd throw that idea out to Detective Hatcher if and when he updated us on the investigation.

BUT THE UPDATE that came wasn't the one I wanted. Around lunchtime, Bo arrived at the cafe, which was unexpected since it was his day off. Even more concerning, he didn't even bother greeting the baristas, but instead headed straight toward the Barks section to sit next to me.

With no preamble, he said, "We've got a problem."

I patted the tiny, shivering shelter dog that had hunkered behind my leg the moment Bo strode in. Sometimes my brother forgot how his dominant personality could fill up a room—especially a roomful of dogs, who naturally revered the leader of the pack.

Unsure how things could get much worse, I asked, "What's up?"

"Detective Hatcher has to bring Vera in for questioning," he said.

"*What?*" I practically shouted. The shy dog leaned against my leg, her body quivering. I'd managed to scare her even more. Understandably, she skittered back a little when I extended my hand to comfort her.

Bo gave a disbelieving shake of his head. "They found Rashana's phone lying on a bank, up a little way from where her body got snagged. It only had her fingerprints on it. But the data retrieval people worked on it all night, and they found a text from Vera." His tone was incredulous. "It appears she asked Rashana to meet her at a certain marker on the trail that day."

My arms felt like they were getting numb as fury built in me. "That can't be right. There's no way Vera would go out on that trail in the cold. She doesn't like getting chilled. That doesn't make a bit of sense."

"I agree, but Charlie had to call her in. I think Randall's bringing her to the station now."

The situation was completely unjust and ridiculous. "Maybe now's the time to call her kids. They need to know what's going on, don't you think? If their mother is one step away from doing jail time at Christmas, they could at least have the decency to come to town and be there for her," I said.

"I'm not sure about that," he said. "We don't know what their relationship is, you know? It's clear she loves them to pieces, but they don't seem to contact her often." He took a deep breath as a customer entered the Barks section and began petting one of the other dogs. "Anyway, we don't even know how to reach them."

I extended a hand again, finally managing to pat the little dog's head. I hoped she might come out to meet the customers. "I appreciate that Randall took Vera to the station. She needs all the support she can get."

Bo nodded. "I'm making salmon and rice tonight—I'll drop some by her place later on. Maybe you could come to my house around seven and have supper with me."

"Okay, but are you sure Vera won't wind up in a jail cell in the meantime?" I asked.

"With Vera, we know we're operating from a foundation of innocence," he said. "The truth will prevail."

But sometimes it didn't, and we both knew that.

VERA GAVE me a call at the end of my work day, her tone defeated. "Would you want to drop by my place sometime? I'm around now." She didn't elaborate, but she didn't have to. Like a good neighbor, I already knew what was going on.

"Of course I do. I'll be over in a minute." After letting Coal out for a quick garden run, I put him back in the house and headed over.

Vera welcomed me at the door, Waffles at her side. Although she tried to sound chipper as she said hello, her face was drawn, as if she hadn't eaten all day.

I gave her a long hug, then pulled back to look at her. "Did Bo tell you he's bringing supper tonight?"

"He did, bless his heart. I appreciate that so much. Randall offered to pick something up, but I can't stomach fast food right now, and that's all he ever gets." She walked into the living room and sank into a chair. For once, Waffles was calm, sitting down next to Vera's slippers.

I took a seat next to her. "What on earth happened? Bo told me you had to go to the police station?"

"They said I'd texted Rashana, but I didn't." It sounded like she was taking short, fast breaths, and for a moment, I worried she might be having heart palpitations. But she rallied, and her tone turned fierce. "The text didn't even come from my phone, of course. They traced it to some kind of burner phone. I assured the detective that I don't even know *where* to get a burner phone, much less how to use one. I can barely use the cell phone I have."

That was certainly the truth. She always had to ask me to load her latest word game apps or to remind her how to turn on location services. I'd always felt her lack of techie skills was amusing, and since I could attest to her ineptitude, maybe that would play into her favor. "What did the text say?" I asked.

She twisted her lips. "It said I'd seen something suspicious on the night of the party that I wanted to discuss with her. But why would I have driven all the way over to that outdoor trail just to talk? That doesn't make sense. If I had anything serious to discuss, I would've just asked Rashana over to my place."

"Of course you would have. But that text makes it sound like you wanted to get her alone in a private area so you could attack her."

She gave an irritated snort.

"It sounds so far-fetched," I said. "Did the detective seem to believe you?"

"I think he did, but the stinky thing is, I don't have a great alibi. I was at home taking a nap about the time they said Rashana was stabbed."

"You didn't talk to Randall or anyone beforehand?"

She shook her head. "No, he was out working. I've been feeling wiped out ever since Goldie's death, so these past few days, I've just kind of fallen asleep come mid-morning."

I knew Vera was under a lot of stress lately, but that level of lethargy was a bit alarming. "Maybe you should get a checkup with Doctor Stokes," I suggested. Stan Stokes was the town's family practice doctor, and he'd been my doctor ever since I was a child. I was sure he was due to retire soon, but I dreaded that day. His wealth of experience and wisdom in making the right calls was unparalleled.

She shrugged. "I probably will. I'll admit I'm not feeling myself."

I tried to hide my concern. "Have they found the knife yet?" I asked.

"No. The detective said they've combed the woods, but they'll be checking the river next."

Waffles lifted her curly head from her paws and gave a long yawn. "I guess she needs to go out," Vera said.

"I'll take her." After walking Waffles to the back door and releasing her into the fenced yard, I returned to the living room. Vera offered me a wan smile. "Would you care for some tea?" she asked.

"I should be asking you that," I said. "Do you want any?"

She shook her head. "I just don't understand what's going on."

One thing was becoming crystal clear to me—someone was trying to frame Vera. There was no other explanation for that text to Rashana.

A few moments later, Waffles scratched on the back door, so I let her in. She raced into the living room and gave Vera an anxious look before plopping down on the floor. I was somewhat comforted to know that Waffles, spastic as she was, seemed to understand that Vera was down. The doodle would definitely try to protect her if anyone showed up at the house with bad intentions.

Although Randall, Bo, and I would be looking in on Vera, it couldn't hurt to have someone staying in the house with her, just in case. I had someone in mind for the job.

"Vera, would you give me your children's phone numbers? I feel they should know what's going on."

"Oh, no, honey, we don't need to concern them," she said. "I'm sure this will all blow over soon."

I hated to put pressure on the older woman, especially in her exhausted condition, but I knew if my mom were entangled in a murder investigation, I'd want to know. "They might want to be here for you—we have to at least give them that chance," I explained.

She looked thoughtfully at the white lights on her Christmas tree. "You know, it's been years since we've spent a holiday together. Maybe they would like to come." She eased up from her chair, then headed for the kitchen. After pulling a well-worn address book from a drawer, she handed it to me. "You'll find their numbers in here. My daughter is named Neva and my son's name is Oren. Neva's married name is Marquez. She's out in Arizona, so she'd have to fly home, but Oren is in Georgia, so it might be easier for him to make it."

Instead of taking her entire address book with me, I said, "Do you mind if I just take photos of the addresses? It'll save me writing it all down."

"Oh, of course. Why didn't I think of that?"

I took photos of the page, knowing that even if they didn't come in this time, it would be handy for me to know how to reach them in the future. Giving the book back to Vera, I said, "I'm going to head home, but call me if you hear anything. Bo will bring your supper over in awhile, and I'll let you know what I hear back from your kids."

"Thank you so much." She gave me a hug.

"Also, I plan to drop by tomorrow on my lunch break. You're not going to escape our Hatfield hospitality." I grinned. "And please try to get in to see Doctor Stokes—I'm happy to give you a ride over."

"I'll tell you when I get an appointment," she said. "Thank you, sweetie."

I gave Waffles' ear an encouraging rub. "You take care of this special lady," I whispered.

The Labradoodle cocked an ear, as if she were taking what I said into consideration. I could only hope the ditzy dog would keep watch over Vera when she was alone tonight.

13

ater on, after Bo had delivered Vera's food, we
settled at his table for some parmesan-crusted
salmon. Coal and Stormy were lying near the
fireplace, dozing in its warm light.

Once I'd scooped a giant helping of herbed rice onto
my plate, I shared details of the text police had found on
Rashana's phone.

Bo frowned. "Vera's the type of person who would call
Rashana if she'd seen anything fishy—she definitely
wouldn't text." He rubbed his red beard. "Then again, if we
boil that text down, there might be a kernel of truth in it."
As if anticipating my defensive reaction, he hurried to
explain. "Of course, we know Vera wasn't the one who
texted. But something about what that text *said* spooked
Rashana enough that she showed up to meet the person
she thought was Vera on the trail."

"And that person stabbed her," I said. "So you're saying
Rashana might've worried Vera had seen her doing something suspicious in the house the night Goldie died?"

"Exactly. Maybe she realized she'd been found out."

I savored another bite of the buttery salmon and let things sink in. "So maybe Rashana somehow gave Goldie an overdose that night...to take over her mayor position, do you think? Would that be a strong enough motive?"

"For some people it might be. I mean, look how desperately Emory Gill wants that position." He took a drink of water. "Another possibility is that Rashana found out Goldie was involved in drug trafficking, so she killed her in order to clean up the town."

"Vigilante justice, huh? I don't know. Rashana didn't strike me as that type. She actually seemed protective of Goldie when Nancy tore into her, not like she had some kind of moral axe to grind with her. I'm just not buying the idea that Goldie was a drug dealer." I chewed another bite of salmon, then washed it down with tea. "Do you think Charlie seriously believes Vera's a suspect in Rashana's murder?"

"He hasn't contacted me tonight, so I'm not sure what other leads he might be following up on. But the reality is that yes, given that text, Vera could be a suspect. I don't think that line of inquiry will go anywhere, but Charlie has a duty to look into it."

I inhaled deeply. "The more I think about it, the more preposterous it seems. Rashana must've had at least seventy-five pounds on Vera—maybe more like a hundred. There's no way our teensie neighbor could've stabbed Rashana with a clean in-and-out move without a serious struggle. In fact, Rashana could've easily grabbed Vera and toppled *her* into the river."

"Good point, though I'm sure Charlie's considered that, too." He stood to clear the plates. "You want some decaf coffee? I have two pieces of Charity's strawberry cheese-cake that she forced me to bring home for us."

"Oh, how mean of her." I smiled. "Sure. Hit me up with some coffee, bro." I glanced at my phone and groaned. "Still no response from Vera's kids. It's so odd."

"They're in different time zones, right?"

"Not her son. Her daughter's in Arizona, but it's daytime there. Bottom line is, they both should've seen the text by now."

He ground beans, and the smell wafted my way. "I know you want to make this thing hunky-dory for Vera, but it might not work out that way. We don't know anything about her children, or even much about her dead husband, really."

"She once told me her husband had gotten tangled in some kind of scam, but she and Auntie A went undercover and busted it wide open. I thought it was quite brave of them. Anyway, she said her husband hadn't been the best dad up to that point, but then he really changed for the better. Maybe her kids only remember his difficult years?"

He brought my coffee over and set it in front of me. "Sure, that's possible. Maybe they hold their dad's behavior against Vera, though I can't imagine why."

"Sometimes people do things that aren't logical, especially when emotions get involved." I took a bite of the cheesecake and breathed a sigh of delight. "Charity is worth her weight in gold," I said.

He nodded. "She could open her own bakery, but I'm glad she has no inclination to do that."

"And no time. She keeps busy with her little sweetie Roman." Charity had recently adopted her five-year-old grandson, and he was a whirlwind of activity.

As Bo finished his last bite of cheesecake, his phone buzzed, so he picked it up. I could tell it was Charlie on the other end. When Bo said goodbye, a relieved smile played at his lips.

"Good news. Vera wasn't the only person texting with Rashana. They found a text from Rashana to Nancy. She said she'd been thinking about things all weekend and couldn't understand why she'd seen Nancy in that room. She and Nancy agreed to talk on Tuesday evening at Barks & Beans."

I felt a stab of sadness that Rashana had planned to patronize our cafe on the night of her death.

"Charlie figures Rashana intended to meet Vera earlier on Tuesday to find out what she knew. Then she planned to approach Nancy with her suspicions," he continued.

"What if Rashana saw Nancy going into that upstairs bathroom and decided to blackmail her? I wonder if she would've been capable of that?"

"It's hard to guess what anyone's capable of, given the right motivation. Charlie plans to bring Nancy in tomorrow morning for questions, but we can't tell Vera about this until that interview is over and we have something more concrete."

Stormy rose and stalked over to my side, making the kind of trilling meow that said she wanted to be picked up.

Coal sat up straighter, but didn't intervene, so I picked Stormy up and stroked her long, soft fur. She started purring in earnest, her bright green eyes focused on me.

"She seems to have toned down some," I said, remembering all too well how she'd knocked the drain hose out of my washing machine and flooded my laundry room the last time I cat-sat her for Bo.

He snorted. "Looks can be deceiving, trust me. She still tries to live up to her name. But I do love her spunk." He reached over and ran a finger along her nose, and she dipped her back, ratcheting up her purring even more.

Coal stood, likely wondering if things were getting out of hand. "I ought to get on home," I said, easing Stormy to the floor. "But what are you thinking about the mayor position? Titan suggested you wait until Rashana's murder is cleared up, at least."

"He called me about that," he said. "I've talked with Summer about it, and while she has some misgivings, it also seems the city needs someone like me as mayor, now more than ever. I'm in close contact with Charlie, so it makes sense that I step in as a kind of city liaison while everything is up in the air." He gave me a reassuring look. "You know I can take care of myself, my little sis."

I wasn't so easily put off. "There's a murderer on the loose, my big bro. I don't care how skilled you are, there's always a chance you could get sideswiped by someone you didn't see coming. Please hold off a few more days, at least."

He shrugged. "I'll see what tomorrow brings."

I worked until lunch Thursday, then I had the rest of the day off to do a little Christmas shopping. I tried to shop local every chance I could, so I bundled up and headed down the snow-dusted sidewalk toward my favorite antique shop, hoping to discover some goodies for family and friends.

The moment I stepped into the cheery brick shop, I

heard a familiar—and grating—voice in the side room. It seemed Matilda Crump was also on the prowl for gifts today.

"I don't care for that shade of red on you," she said loudly.

Another woman murmured something in reply. I darted toward a corner of the shop just as Matilda and Lena Schneider emerged from the room.

The shop owner walked my way. "Could I help you find anything?"

I shook my head, hoping she wouldn't draw attention to me. "Just looking," I practically whispered.

Matilda's head jerked up. Even with her thick glasses, she managed to pin me with her stare. "Macy! I thought I heard you over there."

She walked my way, toting a ghastly looking Christmas doll. I'd like to think the thing had seen better days, but given the terrifying smirk on its baby face, I was afraid it had been designed that way.

With a red crocheted cap in hand, Lena trailed along behind Matilda. I was betting the cap was the red object Matilda had disapproved of, so I was glad Lena had decided to disregard her friend's sideways insult and buy it anyway.

Matilda held the doll out toward me, and I reflexively took a step back. "This is for my collection," she said. "He's worth a pretty penny."

For a moment, I was at a loss for words. Then I managed, "How...unusual he is."

Lena shot me a conspiratorial grin behind Matilda's back, and I felt a sudden kinship with her. How had these two even become friends in the first place?

"Did you hear the news?" Matilda continued. To my relief, she tucked the doll beneath her arm.

"What news?" I knew I was opening myself up for anything, but maybe she could somehow prove helpful.

"They took Nancy Gill down to the police station this morning. It was something to do with her throwing a cat amongst the pigeons at Vera's."

Confused, I said, "Throwing a cat amongst the pigeons?"

She gave me a flippant wave, as if I were an utter imbecile. "I'm talking about how that crazed dog of Vera's was let loose among the guests. The police guessed it was some kind of distraction, and Nancy admitted she opened the crate. She told me as much when I phoned her once she'd said her piece at the bobbies."

I cringed at her British term for the police, but I supposed it was better than saying "po-po." But she wasn't finished yet.

"Did you hear about Rashana Evans?" Matilda continued. "They found her lying stabbed down by the river, can you imagine?"

I certainly could, given that Summer and I were the ones who found her, but I didn't want to give Matilda any fresh fodder. I gave a sad nod. "I've heard."

Cutting a sharp look behind her, she said, "Time to toddle home, what say, Lena?"

Lena smiled. "You go ahead and check out, Matilda. I'll be right there."

Matilda headed for the counter, but she seemed a bit dubious of Lena's intent. The moment she was out of earshot, Lena said, "I know she comes on strong, but she's only trying to protect me."

I turned to the shelf behind me, pretending to browse. "Protect you from what?" I asked quietly.

"I gave Goldie a glass of eggnog that night," Lena said serenely. "I swore I didn't to the police, but Matilda saw me do it. She won't mention it aloud, but I know she's worried about me."

Nearly dropping the jade figurine I had picked up, I turned to look her in the eyes. "Don't you think that's important?"

Matilda glanced up from writing her check and shot us a worried glance.

"It's not, because I didn't put drugs in the eggnog, or whatever it was that killed her."

It hadn't been released in the news that Goldie had died from an overdose, just that her cause of death was under investigation. Lena seemed to know too much, but knowing Matilda, she might have somehow heard about the drugs, then shared that information with her friend.

Matilda grabbed her bag with a loud, "Cheerio," then walked our way. Lena gave me a knowing look, then headed over to buy her red cap.

I turned back toward the shelf. Hopefully, Matilda would take the hint that I needed to do some shopping.

"Tell Vera I'll be looking in on her soon," she said.

I wanted to snidely ask if that was a promise or a threat, but I restrained myself. "Will do."

When I didn't say anything further, Matilda seemed to give up and headed back toward Lena. As the two friends walked out of the shop, I had to admit that even though I truly believed Lena was a good person, she could be a villain who was hiding in plain sight.

Maybe she'd gotten upset over the idea that her

husband was sneaking around with Goldie, so she'd decided to drug a glass of eggnog and hand it to her. It wasn't a stretch to assume Lena would have access to rainbow Fentanyl through her husband's rehab program, since they might've confiscated drugs from the incoming residents.

I hurriedly chose a few gifts, then called Detective Hatcher on the walk home. I told him about my conversation with Lena and suggested he might want to look into her movements a bit more closely.

"Thank you for letting me know," he said. "I'll check into Lena, but we're actually following up on something else right now."

"Nancy Gill?" I guessed.

"Yes, she's involved. Your brother told you about Rashana's text to her?"

"He did. And Matilda just told me she'd talked to Nancy when she got home from the station. She said Nancy was the one who opened Waffles' crate. Why on earth would she do that?" I unlocked my door and let Coal into the garden, then hurried inside to get warm.

"You're not going to like this," he warned.

"Oh, no. Tell me this has nothing to do with Vera," I said.

"I wish I could. Nancy says that Randall Mathena texted her instructions as to what to do if she wanted Emory to get a shot at being mayor. These instructions included opening the dog crate at a specific time."

"This is like a nightmare." I plopped into my chair, pulling a blanket over my legs. "This can't be right."

"Like I said, we're looking into it," he said. "Randall will be coming in soon for some questions. I don't know if he's told Vera or not."

"Let's hope not," I said grimly.

If it were even possible, things had gone from bad to worse for my neighbor. She had precious few support people in her life, and now her boyfriend had been knocked out of that position. Since neither of her ingrate children had responded to my texts, I knew it was up to Bo and me to surround Vera with the same kind of loving care she so willingly lavished on us.

I called up my brother and laid out my plan.

14

"**B**ut why do you have to stay overnight?" Vera asked me a second time. She was scurrying from one kitchen cabinet to the other, setting out the makings of spaghetti for her supper.

I explained things again, glossing over the fact that Randall had jumped on the fast track to becoming a suspect in Goldie's death. "Detective Hatcher needed to ask Randall some questions, just like he did everyone else at the party. Bo and I wanted to make sure you're safe if Randall can't come to see you tonight."

"But he wasn't even planning to drop by." She broke noodles in half, then dumped them into boiling water. "I'm certain I'll be all right on my own—I do have Waffles, you know. What's really going on here, Macy?"

I should've known my insightful neighbor would see through my sham. "There have been some developments in regard to Goldie that might be dangerous for you." This was partially true. Since Randall was involved in trying to take Goldie down, he might try to hit Vera up for an alibi. I didn't want her getting tainted by whatever scheme he'd been in on.

It was disturbing to think that both Nancy and Randall had thought nothing of bringing about Goldie's downfall during Vera's book club party. Whether they had murdered her or somehow set her up to overdose on her own drugs was hardly the point. They had carelessly hung Vera out to dry, and therefore they weren't fit to be anywhere near her, in my mind.

"Okay, hon, if you think it's for the best. I hope you plan to eat here. I have some garlic bread in the freezer, and there'll be plenty of pasta for the both of us."

"Sounds good. I'll get my things. Bo will be staying at my place to let Coal in and out until I come home."

I wasn't sure what day that would be, because I didn't plan to leave Vera alone until Randall's involvement was thoroughly explained.

She gave me a thoughtful look. "I'm not sure what you're up to, but I'm positive you have my best interests at heart." She took the pot over to the sink to drain it. "Your Aunt Athaleen would be proud."

Bo was watching some kind of Nordic mystery when I got home to pick up my things. He'd always been able to handle darker TV themes than I could, and this show was no exception. When he paused the screen, the bleak scenery and the detective's gloomy face clearly conveyed that the world was pain and that there was no relief from it.

"I don't know how you watch that stuff," I grumbled, heading upstairs to pack a bag. "I couldn't sleep at night."

Bo said, "Believe it or not, I find it comforting, since criminals are always brought to justice. It's not always the same in real life. Speaking of which, we need to talk when you're done."

"Oh, great." I sighed, stuffing my clothes and toiletries into a small bag. Coal, who'd followed me upstairs, walked over to his pillow and gave it a longing look.

"It's not time for bed, boy. Bo's going to stay with you tonight. I have to go to Vera's."

Coal's eyes brightened, as if perhaps I might want to take him along.

"No, bud, you're here tonight," I said. It hit me that the days were slipping by fast to Christmas. What a time for Vera to have a murder investigation swirling around her.

Titan was supposed to arrive in two days. I'd already picked up an antique fishing tackle box for his main Christmas gift, but I needed to shop for a little something else. My go-to present for friends, a gift card to the cafe, wouldn't work for my Virginia boyfriend.

After grabbing my bags, I tromped downstairs. "What did we need to talk about?" I asked.

Once again, Bo paused his Nordic show and turned to me. "Have a seat."

That didn't bode well, but I went ahead and sat down across from him. Coal was excited to see me sticking around, so he stretched out on the floor and dropped his large head onto my feet.

"He doesn't want you going anywhere," Bo observed.

I didn't want to prolong my distress. "Tell me what's going on," I demanded.

"I wanted to fill you in on what Charlie told me about Nancy's story," he said. "Something's not adding up—and to me, it seems like Randall is the one piece that doesn't fit."

"If only," I said. "I feel so disappointed in him. But I can't bring myself to tell Vera what he did."

Bo leaned back on the couch. "Nancy claims she received a text from Randall telling her if she wanted her husband to have another shot at being mayor, she needed to help him bring Goldie down. In order to do that, she had to pick up a bottle of pills on her way to Vera's house on the night of book club. They were hidden in a flowerpot just outside Vera's yard. Then, during the party, she was supposed to slip them into the mayor's interior coat pocket. Randall's text described the mayor's coat, down to the last detail, and stated that it would be placed under all the other coats."

I groaned. "This isn't sounding good at all. That coat was the last one left on the bed, and Randall was the one to point it out to the detective. He could've been trying to draw attention to it."

"Maybe." Bo continued. "Nancy also said the text instructed that when she received a text in book club, she was supposed to slip into the guest room and unlock the dog's crate so it could get out."

"Also something only Randall would know—that Waffles' crate was in the guest room," I said.

Coal groaned, shifting his head off my feet. I wiggled my toes, trying to get the blood flow going again.

"Nancy told the detective that Rashana must've seen her going into the guest room around the time Waffles got out. So Rashana texted Nancy that she wanted to meet—probably to blackmail her, Nancy figured."

"Maybe...but what if Rashana just wanted to give her a chance to explain herself before going to the police?"

Bo shrugged. "Unfortunately, we can't be sure what Rashana's motives were. But Nancy swore to the detective that she never went upstairs the entire night. She says she had no idea the mayor was dead until she heard it later from Matilda."

With her continual inside scoops, Matilda should go to work for the local paper, but then again, most of what she reported on would be hearsay.

"Still, if Nancy thought it was a blackmail scenario, she might've met up with Rashana at the park and whacked her, just to keep her husband's name clear."

Sighing, Bo said, "That's the thing. Nancy had an airtight alibi. At the time of Rashana's stabbing, Nancy was all the way over at Pipestem Park, participating in a special 2-hour watercolor class. It's at least an hour and forty minutes to drive from Pipestem to the Greenbrier River Trail. There's no way she could've done both, so I'm inclined to believe her."

"This whole thing sounds carefully planned," I observed. "But the only one who could know the details about Vera's house is Randall."

"I'm not completely sure that's true. Think about it, sis —Vera did book club meetings in her house all the time. Anyone who attended would know that she stored coats on the bed in the guest room, and that she kept Waffles crated in there, too."

"But the drugs in the flowerpot?" I asked.

"That pot sits outside Vera's fenceline, tucked into the

shrubbery along the street. If someone scoped out the place, they could have noticed it and figured it was a good spot to hide things this time of year. No one would disturb the dirt in winter."

I supposed he was right. "Yeah, but it sounds like you're working awfully hard to convince yourself Randall isn't involved."

"To me, he doesn't make sense as a suspect. What would be his motive? He hasn't had any conflicts with the mayor. Also, get this—his text to Nancy didn't even come from his regular cell phone. It was sent from a burner phone." His lips twisted. "Sound familiar?"

"Like Vera's text," I breathed. "You're right. It sounds like someone's setting Randall up, too. Why would anyone target those two? Who could they possibly have ticked off?"

"That's the question I keep asking myself." He stretched. "I just wanted to catch you up on those details."

"Maybe I'm being overprotective by staying over with Vera while Randall's under investigation," I said. "I should probably explain things to her. I doubt he'll try to hurt her in any way."

"It's okay to be protective, but yes, I do think you should explain what happened with Randall so it won't come as a total shock to her."

I stood. "I need to get back over since she was making spaghetti for us. Thanks for filling me in. I need to think through everything."

"That's what I've been trying to do, but things just aren't making sense to me. Let's hope Charlie has a clearer picture."

After giving Coal a kiss and slipping my coat on, I asked, "Did you decide about the mayor position yet?"

He nodded. "I told Cully I'd take it, at least for now. If someone else—obviously not Emory Gill—wants to run for it in the next election, I'm happy to step aside. Provided there's a good candidate for the job, that is."

I gave him a hug. "My brother, saving the world, one small town at a time. I'm proud of you for stepping into the gap. But please be careful, at least until Charlie catches Rashana's killer."

"Of course. Cully's not telling the council until tomorrow anyway."

As I walked to Vera's, I realized I hadn't told Bo how Lena had given Goldie eggnog. Lena had talked about it like she didn't think it was important, so it didn't seem like it was at all significant. But maybe she was putting on a good act. Hopefully Charlie would follow up with her.

I knocked on the door, and Vera shouted for me to come on in. After depositing my bags by the staircase, I took off my coat and boots, then headed for the kitchen. It occurred to me that people in the living room and kitchen couldn't really see into the entryway, given the way the wall jutted out.

It was actually possible that someone could've walked right into Vera's front door during the party when no one was looking. Vera's doors would have been unlocked, since people would've been coming and going from book club. In our small town, the older generation tended to lock doors only when they went out for extended periods of time and when they went to bed at night—Auntie A had been the same.

Bo and I felt a little weird for locking our doors during the daylight hours. But we'd seen too much crime to do otherwise. I'd once urged Vera to follow suit, but she'd laughed it off, saying she had Waffles, and why would she complicate things and lock her door so she had to fumble with the key when she got home, bags in hand?

The police were operating under the assumption that Goldie's killer—if she had one—had slid down the roof, then taken off through the yard in the snow. Maybe they were right.

Vera had already set the table and was pouring red sauce over the noodles. "I hope you like homemade spaghetti sauce. I use my own canned tomatoes." She sighed as she mixed the noodles and sauce. "I'd love to know how many cans your aunt and I put away over the years. I grew the tomatoes—we liked the Romas—and we'd work a day or two for hours on end. It gave us plenty of time to share about our families and our lives."

I grabbed the parmesan from her fridge and set it on the table as she cut the garlic bread. "Macy, I know you're holding back on telling me something. I can see it in those pretty gray-blue eyes of yours. You look sad, and I'd really like to know why."

As we settled into our chairs, I said, "Why don't I pray first, then I'll tell you what's worrying me."

She nodded, so I prayed, then, as we filled our plates, I told her everything I knew about Randall's texts to Nancy.

It was difficult watching Vera react to what I said. Her large eyes got glossy with tears, and her hand froze in front of her face with a forkful of spaghetti wrapped around it.

"But Randall couldn't do that," she protested, finally

moving the cold bite into her mouth. She chewed it so slowly, it was like her jaw wasn't working properly.

I placed my hand on hers. "Bo and I have talked about it, and we don't believe those texts came from Randall."

She gave a small huff. "I can't imagine they did. I mean, if he wanted to let Waffles out of the crate, he could've easily done it himself."

She was right. Randall had been in a far better position to slip in and out of the guest room unnoticed. It didn't make sense he'd ask Nancy to do it.

I'd just sunk my teeth into a slice of garlic bread when the doorbell rang. Vera dusted her hands on her napkin and got up. "I'll get that—you finish your food. I'm afraid I can't eat another bite."

I glanced at the neglected pile of spaghetti and the half-eaten bread slice on her plate. I couldn't bear it if Vera lost her appetite due to my revelation about Randall. I wondered if she was still feeling exhausted, or if she'd gotten an appointment with Doctor Stokes yet.

The sound of voices in the entryway pulled me back into the moment, and I stood. What had I been thinking, letting Vera answer the door on her own? I should've volunteered to do that, instead of stuffing more of her delicious spaghetti in my face.

I hurried into the entryway. Randall was standing in the doorway, deep in conversation with Vera. It was clear from his emphatic hand gestures and his urgent tone that he was trying to convince her that he hadn't sent those texts.

And, given the earnest look in his eyes, I was inclined to believe him.

15

I didn't object when Vera led Randall into the living room. He gave me a kind nod. "You know what's going on, I reckon?"

"I do." I sat down and looked into his eyes—they were, after all, the "windows to the soul," as Auntie A used to say. And Randall's kind eyes looked completely puzzled.

"So you're saying you didn't send the texts to Nancy?" I continued.

He sat down on the couch so carefully, you would've thought it was on fire. I didn't want to make him feel uncomfortable, but then again, there was no way around it. We needed answers.

"Absolutely not. That's what I told Detective Hatcher, too." He turned toward Vera. "I know it sounds unbelievable, since the texts were so specific about things in your house, but I promise you I didn't send them." His face crumpled. "I hate that this has made me look bad to you."

Vera leaned forward and patted his knee. "You aren't tarnished in my eyes, Randall. You just need to hang in there until the police figure out who really sent those texts. Why, even Macy and Bo don't think you did it, and they're regular experts at seeing through liars."

I felt that was stretching it a bit, at least in regard to my ability to spot liars—I had married Jake, after all—but I offered Randall a charitable smile before asking, "Did you know the mayor personally?"

He looked thoughtful. "I'd met her once, at the Christmas parade. But that was before she was mayor. She mentioned how she enjoyed teaching high school English, and I told her a little about my railroad days. She introduced me to Gary, and they seemed really happy together —joking and all. But that was it. I will say I was glad when she won the election—I'd voted for her."

"Anybody in their right mind voted for her," Vera said. "Emory's always been a hothead. I don't know why Nancy supports him like she does."

I felt convinced that Randall was telling the truth. Standing, I said, "Vera, would you mind if I walked Waffles up the sidewalk a bit? That'll give you two time to talk. I know it's dark out, but I'll take my flashlight."

Vera brightened. "Of course. She's been napping in her crate, but you're welcome to take her. She loves the fresh air."

I could tell Vera was pleased that I was leaving her alone with Randall—a sure sign that I trusted him once again. And I did. Randall wasn't a liar, much less a murderer.

As I clipped the leash on a wriggling Waffles, I thought about everyone who'd been at the party that night. Most had been eliminated from suspicion, save Lena, and my gut was telling me she was also on the up-and-up. Doctor

Schneider, too, had a perfectly good reason for visiting Goldie's house, and, as a prominent psychologist, he had no motivation to see one of his clients die.

Waffles bolted out of the house, her claws skittering along the cold porch floor. "Let's not go crazy here, girl," I said, easing down the slippery steps after her. Coal would be utterly appalled if he knew I was walking with his doggie frenemy, practically under his nose. I hoped Bo hadn't chosen this particular moment to let him out into the yard.

To be safe, I headed right, toward Bo's house. The Christmas candles in his windows threw glowing light on Stormy, who was sitting rigidly on her perch, sending us a death glare. I chuckled and raised a hand to her. "Hey, babe," I said.

Waffles gave a short, friendly bark. She had no idea who I was talking to, but she was ready to greet them kindly, all the same. She truly was a "doodle," in all senses of the word. I patted her curly head and continued down the dimly-lit sidewalk.

I needed to clear my head and go back to the beginning of this deathly debacle. I forced myself to picture how the mayor had looked that night, crumpled on the bathroom floor. Of course it was possible she had committed suicide by overdose, but that hardly seemed in character for her. I hardly knew her well enough to make a judgment call, but, from what I'd heard, she and Gary had a good relationship, and she loved her mayor job. She had seemed alert and engaged when leading the book discussion.

Besides, overdosing on illegal Fentanyl hardly seemed a fail-safe method of death. Someone at the party could have found her and administered Narcan, which might have thwarted her attempt. I knew some people in town carried it, due to the level of opioid abuse in the county.

Then there was the whole issue of the drug runner Goldie had spoken with on the trail. It really could have been a complete coincidence that she'd bumped into the girl, and not a calculated drop.

Waffles darted to the right, hoping to chase something that rustled in a nearby yard, but luckily I'd held tight to her leash. Knowing her luck, it was probably a skunk.

"Come here," I said. The dog reluctantly slunk back toward me, and we resumed our walk.

As we reached the final street lamp, I circled around to head back the way we came. Waffles seemed eager to beat a path toward home, so she yanked on the leash again, nearly pulling it from my hand.

"Calm down," I warned. "Or you're going to have to sit a little."

Waffles sidled up close, as if urging me forward. "Okay, let's go," I said. "I don't know about you, but I'm getting cold."

As we got closer to Vera's place, Randall's truck pulled out. He and Vera had likely made peace, and I was glad. He obviously cared for my friend, and not just a little.

But as I got closer, I saw Vera's living room light was out, leaving just the Christmas tree twinkling. Had she already gone to bed? Concerned, I hurried up the stairs and rang the doorbell, which sent Waffles into a frenzy of barking.

Vera opened the door, and even in the dim light, I could tell she was smiling. Maybe she'd been enjoying the ambiance of her tree lights.

But she spoke excitedly. "Macy, I have someone I want

you to meet." Taking Waffles' leash, Vera led me into the living room, where I could now see she'd lit her gas fireplace. Someone rose from the couch and headed toward me.

As the shorter woman came into view, I knew without asking who it was. Her brown eyes were a mirror image of Vera's, and her clothing and shoes were practical, even though her jangling silver bangles and clanking turquoise rings had a Southwestern flair. She looked to be a bit younger than I was, probably in her early thirties.

"Macy, meet Neva. She's my daughter."

I shook Neva's hand. Although I wished she'd let us know she was flying in, I was just thankful she'd shown up for her mom. "It's so good to meet you. I could've picked you up at the airport, if I'd known you were coming."

Neva smiled, flipping her long, dark blonde hair over her shoulder. "I like the drive home, actually, so I just rented a car. I'm sorry I didn't give you a heads-up I was coming. Once I got your text, I had to rearrange some things with my shop and figure out the fastest flights to get me here from Arizona. It was kind of a whirlwind."

"Is your brother coming, too?" I asked.

"I don't think so," she said. "Oren's CEO at a healthcare company in Georgia, so he rarely takes vacation time."

"Don't I know it," Vera muttered.

"Mom." Neva's voice was filled with something akin to teenage attitude. "Don't launch into a guilt trip."

"I hadn't dreamed of it." Vera grinned. "Now, come in the kitchen and let me heat you up some spaghetti."

Realizing Neva would want to crash in the guest room, I said, "You know what? I think I'll head on home, if that's okay with you, Vera. You and Neva need to catch up without me in the way."

Vera shot me a look. "Are you sure? Because you're welcome to stay. You've been such a help to me."

"I'm sure. You all have fun." I headed into the entryway, picked up my things, and walked back home, my heart filled with joy. Vera had gotten her wish this Christmas season—to see one of her children again.

16

S ince Vera was in safe hands, I slept like a log. When my alarm went off, I wasn't ready to roll out of bed and into my Friday work schedule, but Coal came over and nudged my hand. It was his dog duty to be my backup alarm, and he took it quite seriously.

My heart was still light as I got ready and headed over to meet the shelter dogs of the day. Neva would take good care of her mom, and Vera would enjoy showing her around town, I expected. Maybe she'd even bring her by Barks & Beans at some point.

LENA SCHNEIDER CAME into the cafe after lunch, looking snappy in her businessy black trousers, ivory turtleneck, and leather high-heeled boots. She purchased a few bags of coffee, then walked over to the Barks section to say hello. I was struck again by her beauty—given her bone structure, she could be some kind of model.

"I'm sorry I had to cut our conversation short at the antique shop," she said. "Matilda—well, you know her. She often has her own agenda. But, as I was saying, she means well."

The dogs tore around in a small circle on the front mats as I asked, "Could you tell me when you gave Goldie that eggnog?"

"Let's see. I got up toward the end of Goldie's talk and poured myself a glass. About that time, Nancy insulted Goldie by saying she must be good at tallying votes, so I figured I'd pour some eggnog for Goldie, too. I was hoping to soften Nancy's rudeness, I suppose. I handed it to her when the discussion ended. That must've been right before she went upstairs."

I must've been captivated by the hostilities between Nancy and Goldie, because I hadn't even noticed Lena get up at that point, much less hand Goldie eggnog.

But there was really no way around it—the glass that Lena handed Goldie had to be the same one that had shattered soon after on the bathroom floor, laced with fatal drugs.

Realizing I was staring at Lena like she was a criminal, I shifted my gaze toward the frolicking dogs. I took a moment to compose my thoughts, then said, "Lena, to be honest, you gave me the impression you were attacking Goldie yourself during the book discussion. You made that comment about affairs coming to light, and it seemed pointed toward the mayor. So I'm not sure why you'd offer her a glass of eggnog to comfort her for Nancy's insult."

Lena adjusted the strap of her soft-looking leather tote. "I'll admit I was upset with Goldie earlier that night. Matilda had told me something that made me distrust her.

But when I made my comment about the affairs, Goldie seemed genuinely bewildered as to what I meant. I realized Matilda must've gotten her wires crossed somehow." She gave a half-grin. "It wouldn't be the first time, trust me. Anyway, by the end of the discussion, I felt uncomfortable with the way Nancy was behaving toward Goldie."

Either Lena was telling me the truth, or she was an expert at spinning things in her favor. It was hard to tell, but I knew her husband fairly well, and I didn't think he would have married a liar. Or a narcissist, for that matter. Lena's angelic face looked incapable of malice.

Then again, so had Jake's, and he'd been running around on me.

I wished I had time to ask Bo over to talk, since he was a better judge of character than I was, but Lena was already turning to leave. "Thank you again for introducing me to your delicious coffee," she said. "I bought some beans as gifts for my children this year. They're real coffee fiends. I'll be sure to send them here for a visit while they're in."

She definitely knew how to butter me up—by complimenting our wares and supporting our cafe.

"Thanks so much." I watched as she walked out the door. As Christmas tunes played softly in the background, I wondered if Detective Hatcher was going to ask Lena some questions. I was no good at seeing through someone who seemed so genuine.

Bo picked me up in his truck at four, so we could get to the tree farm while it was still light. We had to wind up several back roads to reach the open, hilly space that harbored a variety of well-tended evergreens.

I cranked Christmas music as he drove, another tradition we'd clung to through the years.

"I was thinking of a Fraser fir," he said. "I've heard they're hypoallergenic."

I shot him a look, but his gaze was fixed on the curves ahead. "I don't have allergies."

"I know, but maybe they're better for our pets."

"Okay, but do our pets have allergies?" I asked sweetly.

He made a right turn, onto the long, one-lane drive to the farm. "Why do I have the feeling this isn't going to be a fast process?"

"Picking the perfect tree isn't all about 'fast,' you know."

He grinned as he parked in the gravel lot. "No, but we'd better pick them before it gets dark."

Bing Crosby had just launched into the chorus of "Silent Night" when I had to turn off my phone. Bo pushed his seat forward, then grabbed his gloves and hacksaw from the back.

It seemed that every year we came to the tree farm, the sky was the same icy gray shade, dotted with steely gray clouds. A drizzle of rain peppered our hats, but it was easily brushed off. The land was bleak and beautiful, and standing on top of the tree-covered hills always made me feel like some kind of highland lass.

"Earth to Macy," Bo said, interrupting my Scottish musings. "What about that one, over there?" He pointed to a smaller fir that looked too sparse to me.

"I'd like something bigger for my place," I said. "Maybe you could get that one for yours?"

He looked dubious. "I think I'll check out a few more

first," he said. "What if I look through the firs, and you can head over to the spruce section so we can save time."

"I'm actually thinking pine," I said. "Big, fluffy white pine branches that smell like Christmas. Those are the next hill over. I'll go that way."

"I'll come and find you once I've cut mine," he said.

I walked along the snow-smashed, yellowed grass until I found the pine section. I was examining a medium-sized tree when someone called out to me.

"Hi there. You're out here getting a tree too, huh? I was just on my way to get this one wrapped."

Cully Stone walked my way, dragging a smaller pine behind him. He wore tan Carhartt coveralls and a cap with The Greenbrier logo on it. I wondered if he golfed in his spare time, but being a golfer at The Greenbrier couldn't be cheap.

"I am—I didn't get out here as early as I'd hoped this season," I said.

He let the tree drop to the ground. "Things get busy; I understand." He smiled. "I have to say, I was thrilled when Bo agreed to become mayor. I know he'll help steer things the right way. We were getting off-course with Rashana." Catching himself, he said, "I'm sure that sounds horrible. But she really did botch a project that was critical to Lewisburg safety. There was just no way I could've recommended her as mayor."

The light was fading, and I knew I needed to get back to my tree hunt. "I was sorry for how she died, though," I said. "My friend and I found her when we were walking along the river."

Cully's eyes widened. "You were the ones who found her? I'm very sorry. It sounded so brutal." He picked up his tree trunk. "I guess it was a good thing she was wearing a bright hoodie so you saw her."

"That helped, but if her hoodie hadn't gotten caught on a branch, we probably would have missed her, because she would have sunk. Bodies only float after they start to decompose." I stepped toward the tree, then turned as something hit me. "Wait a minute, how did you know she was wearing a bright hoodie that day? I never saw that in the news."

His green gaze sharpened. "I don't know. Bo must've mentioned it to me."

It felt like a punch to the gut, because I knew he was lying.

Even if I'd told Bo what Rashana was wearing—and I couldn't recall that I had—he never would have mentioned it to anyone. He was close-lipped about any and all police business, except with me and Titan.

As dark clouds scudded overhead, my legs wobbled a little on the uneven hill. What was I supposed to do now? Accost him? Accuse him of knowing too much?

Cully hadn't taken a step. He, too, seemed uncertain about what to do next. But then his eyes hardened, and it was clear he'd come up with a solution to my incriminating question.

A deadly solution.

In one swift move, he dropped the tree and lunged for me. I jumped back and took off running up the hill, not daring to look back. Dodging between thick pines, I prayed he wouldn't spot me. Luckily, I'd worn a green coat, so maybe I was somewhat camouflaged.

But he jumped out as I rounded a tree. Since hiding was no longer an option, I screamed at the top of my lungs and tried to duck away. To my horror, he tackled me to the ground, bumping my shoulder into the sharp end of a cut-off tree stump. I yelped in pain.

He fit his gloved fingers around my neck. As he started to squeeze, he said, "I'm so sorry. I didn't want to do any of this. But you're the only one who knows it was me."

Remembering a move Bo had shown me as a teen when he was lecturing me about watching out for pushy boys, I thrust my hips and thighs upward, knocking Cully off-balance. The moment his hold was broken, I grabbed his arm and pushed at his stomach, twisting to escape the weight of his body. At the same time, I shouted as loudly as I could.

Cully tried to grab my neck again, but before he could, a fast-moving body slammed him off me. Struggling to sit up, I saw Bo punch the older man's face before pinning him to the ground. My brother then pulled his tactical knife out of a sheath on his belt and held it toward Cully's throat. "Don't make one move," he said.

Turning to me, he breathlessly asked, "You okay, sis?"

I rubbed my neck. Cully would've had a hard time strangling me with his thicker work gloves on, but he had managed to cause some bruising. "I'm fine."

"Could you call Charlie and tell him we're bringing Cully to the station for a little visit?"

I was already grabbing my phone from my coat pocket. "Of course."

By this time, one of the customers had alerted the tree farm owners. Two men jogged toward us, and together, they tied Cully's hands and feet with tree twine. Then they graciously offered to watch the bound-up city manager while Bo and I chose our trees.

This time, I made fast work of picking a pine. I knew I couldn't let this near-strangulation encounter ruin my delight in the tree farm, but right now, I just needed to get home.

Once the trees were wrapped, we headed toward the lean-to barn where the farmers were holding Cully. I stopped in the open doorway, hesitant to get near my attacker. Bo glanced at me, and I could feel flames of anger as red as his hair emanating from him. He marched toward the man he'd assumed was a friend.

"Care to explain why you were trying to kill my sister?" he asked.

Cully sighed as if he couldn't fight anymore. "You're not going to believe this, but I was doing it all for my grand-daughter."

"What's your granddaughter have to do with anything?" Bo asked.

I crept closer so I could hear Cully's answer, but I made sure to stand just behind my brother's powerful frame.

"They threatened her," he said. "Said if I didn't do what they asked, they'd kill her. They had pictures of her on her school playground in Ohio and everything."

"Who's 'they?'" I cautiously asked.

"I have no idea. It was all done by text. All these demands...I don't know what I've been reduced to." He dropped his head in defeat. "I'm not a murderer. I'm not."

Bo grabbed Cully and pulled him to his feet. "Yet you met their demands, so I'm guessing you've killed some people along the way, haven't you?"

Cully barely nodded as Bo led him to the truck. Someone had already loaded our trees into the bed. "Sis, you sit in the back seat, behind me. Cully will be in the front where I can get to him."

"I'm not going to try anything," Cully said. "My wife is going to divorce me for this. My life is over."

I'd met Cully's wife Sue Ellen once, at a charity event, and she'd seemed very kind. I couldn't help feeling sorry for a man who'd been put in an impossible position—choosing between his granddaughter's life or committing unthinkable crimes. I would have been tempted to make the same decision he had.

"She might forgive you," I said as Bo shoved him up onto the seat.

But as I climbed into the truck, I found myself wishing I didn't have to sit near a murderer. There'd be no Christmas music this trip home from the tree farm.

17

At Bo's request, Detective Hatcher agreed to let us stand behind the mirrored window and watch as they interrogated Cully. "You two caught him for me, so you might as well listen to what he's been up to," he said.

Although I wanted to get home and snuggle up with a glass of warm cider and Coal at my feet, I owed it to Vera to find out the truth. I couldn't tell her much of what we overheard, but if Randall was indeed innocent in Goldie's death, I could at least assure her of that. The detective could fill her in on the other details later.

Cully sipped at a cup of water as an officer pressed a record button, then read him his Miranda rights. Once she'd finished her recital, Detective Hatcher asked Cully if he understood.

"I do, and I want to get this stuff off my chest," Cully said. "I don't care to have a lawyer present." After signing a paper to that effect, he began to explain how someone had threatened his granddaughter if he didn't carry out their orders.

The detective said, "You said you received anonymous texts giving you instructions. If I check your phone, will I find them?"

Cully shook his head. "I couldn't run the risk of leaving them on there, so I deleted them. But I'd imagine there's some way to retrieve them."

"You don't know who sent them to you? They never gave a name?"

"No names. But they'd proved they had my grand-daughter—her name is Nikki—in their sights. I couldn't let them harm her." He gave a small smile. "She's our world."

The detective seemed to soften, but it might have been an act. "I understand. So you felt you had to comply to keep Nikki alive."

Cully gave a silent nod.

"What, specifically, did they ask you to do?" the detective asked.

"First, they told me they were going to drop off a chocolate mint that I needed to offer Goldie at some point during the party. They wanted me to give it to her unnoticed. Then they asked me about the layout of Vera's house, so I described things to them." He paused. "When I mentioned she had a dog, they asked more specific things, like where she kept Waffles and where guests' coats were hung during book club."

So that's how they'd known Waffles was kept in a crate in the guest room—and that the mayor's coat would be lying on the bed. That kind of insider information had made it easy to set Randall up via a burner text to Nancy.

The detective leaned forward. "You said they gave you a chocolate mint. How did they do that? Did you see them?"

Cully shook his head. "Someone dropped it in my mailbox, late at night. I got up early the next morning and retrieved it."

"And you managed to secretly give the mint to Goldie? How did that happen?"

Cully said, "I had to wait in my car for an opportunity to sneak into Vera's house. About ten minutes before the party, when I knew her dog would be in the crate, I worked up the courage to slip up the stairs and hide in a closet."

The detective's brow wrinkled. "But how did you know Goldie would be coming upstairs?"

"I didn't, but since the main guest bathroom was up there, I guessed that she would at some point. It was sheer luck that she was the first person to come up. I did have a backup plan—to give it to her on the sidewalk afterward— but that would've been far more risky since someone might see me."

"How could you be sure she'd eat the chocolate you gave her?" the other officer asked.

Cully's voice was barely above a whisper. "Because she trusted me."

Detective Hatcher seemed to recognize Cully's genuine distress. "Could you walk me through your interaction with Goldie at the book club party?"

"Yes. I waited in the closet until I heard the discussion ending. Then I stepped out of the closet and opened the bedroom door so I could see if Goldie came upstairs. The moment her head came into view, I stepped into the hallway and offered her a chocolate mint. I made some kind of quiet joke about how she probably needed a little treat." He looked like he was trying to compose himself. "She...she didn't even ask me why I'd come. She just took the mint and ate it." He hesitated again. "When her eyes started to close, I grabbed her beneath the arms and shifted her onto the bathroom floor."

"Were you aware there were drugs in the mint?" the other officer asked.

"No. They'd just told me it would knock her out, and to be prepared."

"So you didn't realize it would kill her?" the detective asked.

Cully took a moment to respond. "I kind of figured it might, given how secretive they wanted me to be."

I could feel Bo's body tense next to me. Like me, he was probably wishing Goldie hadn't eaten that mint.

The detective continued. "We found traces of a Fentanyl blend on the shattered glass on the bathroom floor. What can you tell us about that?"

"Goldie had set her eggnog on the banister outside. I didn't want to leave it there to draw attention to where she was. I had a sudden brainstorm that I could use her glass to make it look like she poisoned herself. Like I said, I didn't know what was in that chocolate, but I took the wrapper and rubbed it all over the inside of the glass. Then I wrapped it in the bathroom rug and broke it, so no one downstairs would hear."

"That explains the drugs on the shards," the officer said.

"Did anyone see you doing all this?" the detective asked.

Cully shook his head. "I acted fast and locked us both in the bathroom. Someone did knock on the door soon after, though. A woman, I think. But she left when I didn't respond."

That must've been Rashana, as Dylan had mentioned.

"I thought about climbing out on the roof," Cully said. "I opened the window to see how solid it was, but when I put a hand on it, the snow slid off. I got a little panicky, but someone texted me and said the dog was going to get loose in the house, so the moment people started yelling, I needed to run out the front door. I waited a little longer and, sure enough, I heard screams, so I ran out, then took off in my car."

"That hardly seems like a solid plan," the detective said. "Someone could've seen you."

"I didn't have any choice. Thankfully, it was snowing hard by then," Cully said. "I saw Mark Schneider walk up to the porch just after I'd closed my car door. But he didn't see me."

The other officer leaned back and crossed her arms. "What can you tell us about Rashana's murder?"

Cully's face clouded. "I thought it was all over. They'd assured me that would be all they wanted from me. But a couple days later, I got another text. They said Goldie had died of an overdose, and they could easily plant the drugs that killed her somewhere in my house, then point the police toward me. They demanded I do one last thing for them."

"Rashana," Bo breathed.

Cully spoke quickly. "I couldn't handle harming someone else. I decided to draw my line in the sand, so I texted back that they might as well plant the drugs and call the police on me—I'd tell them the whole truth."

"You really kicked the hornets' nest," the officer said. "What did they say then?"

Cully drooped in his chair. "They said that not only would they kill my granddaughter, but they'd torture her mother—my daughter—in front of her first. Then they sent more photos of my daughter's home."

"This is quite a far-reaching operation," Bo said into the silence of our room.

"And Rashana?" the detective quietly pressed.

Cully's tone was resigned as he nodded. "It was me. I used an old kitchen knife, then buried it afterward in my back yard. It was quite a chore digging into that frozen layer of soil. I told my wife I was planting bulbs, and she didn't know any different, since she's not a gardener." He gave the detective a desperate look. "I knew dead bodies sank at first—I'd read that somewhere. And she would've sunk, too, if the current hadn't pushed her into that branch."

Cully hadn't described the logistics of how he'd met with Rashana and stabbed her, but I was guessing he was blocking the details from his mind. Summer had guessed the murderer hadn't been very committed to his task, and she'd been right. Cully hadn't wanted to do any of it, but he'd seen no way out.

"Why are you talking to us now?" Detective Hatcher asked. "Didn't they threaten to kill your daughter and granddaughter if you squealed?"

Cully shrugged. "I figured I'd go down for murder. I mean, I did it, didn't I? I killed two women, and I thought about killing another just to keep my family safe. No one has to know I said anything about being coerced into it. I'll plead guilty, then I'll go to prison, so they'll have no reason to harm the ones I love."

There didn't seem to be a happy ending to this story, because Cully was right—he *had* killed the mayor and Rashana, and he'd also attempted to strangle me.

Bo drew his eyebrows together. "Something bigger is going on here," he said firmly. "I need to talk with the detective." He sent a brief text, and a moment later, we saw the detective glance at his phone in the interrogation room.

"Give me a minute," the detective said, then strode out.

He walked into our viewing room. "What's up?" he asked. "You heard his confession?"

Bo nodded. "At this point, I think you need to loop the DEA in on things. Whoever these people are, they have a reach into Ohio, and they also have access to rainbow Fentanyl. I suspect they targeted Goldie for a reason. She might've been looking into the drug trade in Lewisburg, tracking people down..." He snapped his fingers. "Like when she met with that drug courier on the trail. She might've been pumping the girl for information, even before she became mayor."

The detective gave a slow nod. "They might've wanted her out from the moment she got in. But we looked through her files and computer records and didn't find any kind of evidence to that effect."

"The people behind this could've gotten to her things before you did. They could've searched her house while she was at the party."

Bo had a point. "But why would they have Cully get rid of Rashana, too?" I asked. "Had Goldie told her about the drug dealers?"

"I don't think so. Rashana was likely killed because she saw Nancy leaving the room around the time the dog got out. She must've put two and two together and realized it was some kind of diversion, and she was probably going to report it to the police—although she might've planned to blackmail Nancy, too. It's hard to say, but the people running this show didn't want the police knowing about Nancy's role in things, even though they'd still covered their bases by making it look like Randall set up the dog release distraction."

"This whole thing has felt very orchestrated," I said.

The detective nodded. "I agree. I'm going to make sure Cully has a good lawyer. Bo, could you contact your friends in the DEA and have them call me?"

"Will do." Bo shot a glance at me. "And Charlie, if you don't mind, I'm taking Macy home now. We have some Christmas trees that need to get in water."

18

Once Bo had secured my pine in the tree stand, I gave it a couple of pitchers of water. Coal gave the tree a final sniff before sinking to the ground in front of it. He would find our new living room "accessory" boring until I hung some ornaments on it, at which point, he'd take it upon himself to chomp down on anything that looked remotely ball-like. For that reason, I'd switched to non-breakable ornaments last year.

Bo, too, had boarded the non-breakable train. Last Christmas, Stormy had zoomed up his tree trunk and knocked the entire thing over. Thankfully, none of Auntie A's antique ornaments had been broken in the process.

I leaned back on the couch. "I can't even think about decorating it until tomorrow," I said. "I'll have time to get things on it before Titan gets here."

"When does he get in?" Bo asked.

"Tomorrow afternoon—and don't worry, he'll be here for your super-secret carriage ride," I said.

The pleased smile on Bo's face eased all the weariness I

was feeling. I knew he couldn't wait to propose to Summer, and I couldn't wait to see the look on her face when he did.

RAIN PATTERED on the eaves as I roused late on Saturday morning. I hoped it wasn't going to discourage Bo from his carriage ride, but we both knew that weather could be fickle in December, so the sprinkles could stop at any time. At least it must've warmed up, since it was rain and not snow falling.

Titan had sent me a text late last night, saying he was heading out of his place in Virginia around one in the afternoon. That would put him here around four, so I had plenty of time to decorate the tree.

As I went up the attic steps to retrieve an ornament-filled bin, Coal sat at the foot of the stairs, watching in case I fell down, I supposed. "You're a good boy," I crooned. "Good baby."

Once I'd lugged the bin downstairs, I launched into my yearly process of sorting through the chaos to find what I needed. First, I located my lights and started stringing them.

But after draping five strands, I realized the final string ended in an outlet instead of a plug, so I had to reverse the entire process and restring. I could've kicked myself for not checking the end plug *before* I'd launched into my lighting venture.

Next, I set out the ornaments. I'd gone with a soft turquoise, purple, and hot pink color scheme. I was a single woman, so why not? Coal gave a nervous lick of his lips when he saw a big pink rocking horse ornament emerge from the bin. It had his tooth marks on it from last year.

I pointed to it, knowing what he was thinking. "This is not for you. *Not for you.*" Getting on my step stool, I hung that one toward the top, although if Coal jumped up, he could easily reach it.

Once I'd "iced" the tree with a sparkly turquoise ribbon, I gave Bo a call. "You want to put the star on for me?"

It was another of our Christmas traditions. When we were teens, Auntie A had always asked Bo to place the angel on top since he was the tallest. When I'd moved out on my own, I'd decided I preferred sparkling star toppers to angels, since I loved contemplating the star of Bethlehem. For years, I'd placed the star myself, then once I was married, I'd had Jake do it. After moving home to Lewisburg, I'd handed Bo his tree-topping job back for sentiment's sake—but mostly because I loved spending time with my brother at Christmas.

"I'll be right over," he said. "You want some pancakes? I made a big batch."

That wasn't an accident, I was sure. He'd been thinking of me this morning—probably wondering if I'd been completely traumatized by my near-strangulation yesterday.

"Of course I want some! Bring them over. I have plenty of maple syrup."

We always stocked up on maple syrup from a friend's farm in March, and I still had some left over from early this year.

It took less than five minutes for Bo to jog up to my door, a plate of pancakes in hand. He set them on the counter, gave me a hug, petted Coal's head, then walked over to place the star. My brother didn't have a slow mode. He either moved fast or he was completely down for the count, like when he got the flu. There were no in-betweens. I loved that about him, but I could never function that way. I'd be out of energy in a day.

"Looks great, sis." He angled the star forward. "Does that seem right?"

"It's perfect," I said. "Did you get yours decorated?"

"Bright and early. I wanted to get it out of the way. I wound up putting most of the ornaments toward the top, where Stormy can't bat them off, so I'm afraid it looks top-heavy."

"No one's going to care," I said. "You know Summer just puts up a fake tree every year, with the ornaments attached to it, since she's always fostering cats."

"I know, but I'm hoping she'll come over to the live-tree side someday." He moved my step stool back to its nook in the kitchen and sat down. "Try some pancakes," he urged.

"I have to heat them up. I'm going to brew some coffee first. You want some?"

"Thanks, but I've already had some. I need to get back over. I'm trying to get everything ready for tonight."

I knew Bo must've run through the proposal scenario in his head a million times already. For important events like this, he liked to be prepared for every possible curveball.

"What're you wearing?" I asked.

He grinned. "I'm wearing that light blue sweater Summer likes on me, and some black jeans and boots. We're going out to eat first."

"That'll look nice," I said. "We'll probably eat out, too. I don't want to have to cook before your big event. Actually —I don't ever want to cook."

He could see through my lighthearted façade. "Are you doing okay today? I forgot to mention that you did great wrangling out from under Cully. If you hadn't done that, I might not have been able to tackle him so easily."

"You taught me all my best moves." I set the plate of pancakes in the microwave.

"I'll head back then," he said. "Enjoy."

"Hang on." I turned. "What's going to happen with the city manager position, now that Cully's not doing it? You're not going to move into that, are you?"

"No way. That's a big responsibility." He looked thoughtful. "To be honest, Cully did take his responsibility seriously, from what I can tell. He was committed to doing things the right way. It's really bizarre that someone would lean on him, of all people, for their own nefarious purposes."

"It reminds me a little of Anakin Skywalker. The fear of losing those he loved outweighed his determination to do what was right." We'd watched many *Star Wars* movies together.

"Well, Anakin was also driven by a lust for power. But someone knew how Cully ticked, and that he would die on the hill of protecting his family."

We both fell silent, knowing we would do the exact same.

Finally, Bo cleared his throat and answered my question. "Mack Lilly is going to step into the city manager position until they can vote someone in. He's already a council member."

"Isn't he a retired lawyer?" I asked.

He nodded. "He's a smart man, and a bit of a hard-hitter, so if someone tries to get to him, they're going to have an uphill battle. In the meantime, the DEA is running down that specific blend of Fentanyl in the mayor's pocket, to see if it links up to a particular dealer. That could point us to the one who's been pulling the strings with Cully."

"And how's Cully's family?" I still felt sorry for the man, who'd had his freedom stripped away by a ruthless—and anonymous—texter.

"His wife Sue Ellen is sticking by his side. Charlie said she came down to the station and Cully explained things to her. She actually told him she would've done the same thing, if she'd known their daughter and granddaughter were in mortal danger." He pulled on his tennis shoes. "I'll get back and let you eat, sis."

"Thanks for putting the star up, and for the pancakes," I said. "See you tonight—what time again?"

"Just meet in front of City Hall at seven-thirty. I've booked the carriage after his regular rides are over, so it'll just be us."

"That's so sweet." A delicious shiver ran down my arms. "This is going to be one of the best days ever, Bo."

THANKFULLY, I had time to run to a nearby shop and pick up some handmade shaving products for Titan's final Christmas presents. I tucked his gifts under the tree, excited to watch him open them.

As planned, he got in just after four. When he knocked on the door, Coal barked a couple of times, but once I opened it, he turned into a whimpering puppy begging for love. I found it cute that my huge boyfriend and my huge dog had bonded so well.

After giving Coal a bit of attention, Titan stepped into my living room and tenderly touched my cheek. A sprinkle of rain fell from his knit cap to my chin as I tipped upward to give him a kiss. He returned it like a man who'd been starved of affection for months.

"I'm glad you're here," I murmured, breathing in the woodsy smell of him.

"Trust me, I am, too. It's been busier than you'd think for the Bureau during the holiday season." A thick brown curl fell over one of his concerned eyes. He often let his hair grow out for the holidays, and I found his curls irresistible. "But tell me everything that happened yesterday. Your text was kind of vague."

Last night, I'd only told him that Bo and I had brought Goldie and Rashana's murderer to the station. I couldn't bring myself to tell him the rest.

But now, with my treetops glistening and my boyfriend listening, I sat on the couch and told him about how our tree farm visit had turned into the kind of nightmarish showdown I'd never dreamed I'd have with an upstanding city manager. Titan's jaw hardened as I mentioned Cully's gloved hands wrapping around my neck, but he relaxed when I said Bo had crashed into the man and taken him to the ground.

"I'm glad they've shifted Cully's case over to the DEA," Titan said when I finished. He was sitting so close, I could see the golden flecks in his light brown eyes, and he'd wrapped an arm around me, as if to protect me from harm. "The drug connection has to be significant."

"That's what Bo thought." I glanced at the clock. "You

want to open gifts before we head out to eat? I know Christmas isn't until next Monday, but you'll be up with your family then."

"I'd love to. I'll run out and get mine." He looked at Coal, who was stretched out in front of the couch. "I even got something for this big guy."

Coal raised his head and gave a happy whap of his huge tail on the rug. My Christmas season had truly started at last, now that I was surrounded by the people I loved.

19

The rain had completely stopped by the time we headed into our favorite Mexican restaurant, and, as we were eating our tacos, the fiery light of a beautiful sunset streamed through the window. "It's going to be a perfect night for Bo's carriage ride," I said.

I'd told Titan of Bo's proposal plans, and he'd been pleased to be included. He'd met Summer a few times when Bo had invited us over for food and board games, and he approved of her. "She's a good balance for Bo," he'd said once. He should know, since he'd partnered with my brother in the past on joint-agency missions.

Darkness had fallen when we parked near City Hall. Bo and Summer were already sitting under a plaid blanket in the covered white carriage, and, once Titan and I had taken our seats across from them, the driver clicked the horse forward. Bells jingled under the horse's neck, lending a festive air to the occasion. Shop windows were dressed for Christmas, and the sidewalks were lit with Christmas lights.

"What a magical night," Summer remarked, snuggling closer to Bo.

She had no idea just how magical it was going to get. I avoided looking at them, in case I was accidentally smirking with all my insider knowledge. I wasn't sure when Bo was going to propose, but it couldn't come soon enough. His secret was burning a hole through me.

Finally, as the carriage pulled to a stop under a streetlamp and the bells stopped their jingling, Bo took a deep breath. I tightened my arm that was looped under Titan's, and he gave it a squeeze.

"Summer," Bo began, turning to look at her. "You...you can't know how much you mean to me. I wish I could explain it. You make me excited to be alive."

The horse shifted a little, and the carriage rocked. Bo took Summer's hand in his and knelt to the floor of the carriage. "I'm proud of who you are and of how you treat the people—and the animals—in your life. You love me so well."

Suddenly, a stench drifted our way. The stench of steaming fresh horse manure.

The driver called back, "I'm so sorry. She doesn't usually go this long without a bathroom break."

Bo's face contorted, then he burst into laughter. Summer gave a kind of chortling snort. "Don't worry about it. I grew up Mennonite, you know. Horse dung is nothing new."

At that quip, I couldn't stop myself. I started laughing so hard, tears rolled down my face. What crazy timing on the part of that horse.

Titan handed me a tissue. Bo managed to compose himself and continued, despite the overwhelming stink.

"I'll speed this up so we can get out. Summer, would you make me the happiest man in the world and marry me?"

She beamed at him. "Yes, of course I'll marry you, Bo Hatfield!"

As Bo pulled the ring box from his coat pocket, I turned on my phone's flashlight so Summer could get a proper look at it. He snapped the lid open, and Summer gasped as the diamond glittered up at her.

"Oh, Bo, it's beautiful," she breathed. As she slipped it on her finger, I began to sob.

She looked over at me. "Oh, Macy, you'll be my sister for real now," she said.

Even as the pungent scent of manure seemed to suck the air out of the carriage, I knew that Auntie A was smiling down on us from heaven. Bo had found the woman of his dreams, and I'd gained the sister I'd always wanted.

WE SAID goodbye to the mortified carriage driver, promising we wouldn't give him any negative online reviews, then we split up. Bo and Summer headed back to his place to celebrate with a dessert Charity had created just for them, and Titan and I climbed into his black SUV to head to the drive-through Christmas lights display on the state fairgrounds. I hadn't done it before, but I was impressed.

As we drove under a long archway curtained with green and white lights, Titan said, "That was a great proposal, even though things didn't quite go according to plan."

"It'll be memorable, that's for sure. But yeah, it was." I felt at a loss for words, but Titan didn't mention it, which I appreciated.

Instead, he reached across the center console and took my hand. "What are your thoughts on that—I mean, on marriage?"

Now I was really at a loss for words. Although neither of us would've entered into a dating relationship if we hadn't believed it could lead to marriage, I wasn't sure if I was ready to dive into matrimonial bonds again.

"Marriage is great," I said, but my tone was utterly unconvincing.

He seemed to get the message. "I know, we both come from divorces where our spouses walked out on us. We have some baggage."

That was an understatement.

"I know I've told you I didn't communicate well with Regina when we were married, and that I kept long hours and traveled too much. But with you, things are somehow so much easier."

He rarely spoke his ex-wife's name. They'd only been married a couple of years when she'd left him, and I secretly believed she'd deliberately guilted him about his work hours to cover for the time she had been spending with the man she'd married next. Titan had an acute conscience, and someone unscrupulous could play on that.

"I agree," I said, trying to encourage him. "You've never had any trouble communicating with me." I smiled.

"Though I'm well-acquainted with the male psyche, after living with Bo all these years."

He slowed the SUV near a grouping of lights. "I love that about you. You never expect me to be poetic or mushy or something I'm not."

I fell silent, looking at the tall pole that had been strung with lights to look like a tree.

He seemed to pick up on my unease and changed the subject. "Bo and I got a text just before our carriage ride," he said. "The DEA got in touch with the FBI, and you're never going to believe what they found in that Fentanyl planted on Goldie."

"I can't even guess," I said. "I'll admit I don't know much about the illegally-concocted drug scene."

He gave me a partial smile, which let me know that whatever news he'd gotten was serious. "They've only seen that blend once before, in the drugs picked up on that drug runner Goldie ran into on the trail. The DEA has finally traced that blend back to Leo Moreau's traffickers in this area."

"But Leo's not at the helm of the ship anymore," I said. "Unless he's selling drugs from prison."

"We keep a tight rein on him, so that's really impossible." Titan glanced my way before steering toward the fairground exit. His eyes were dark.

I suddenly realized what he meant. "You're saying someone else is running Moreau's drugs through our town. Let me guess—our favorite southern belle has graduated from art fencing to running her husband's more destructive enterprises. Anne Louise Moreau is now an official drug dealer."

"It appears that way," Titan said. "She managed to drop

off our radar last week. It was like she knew things were coming to a head here."

I sighed. "How would you feel about playing some video games with me tonight? I think I need to blow off some steam."

"I'll watch you play. Remember, I have to use a large-sized controller."

I looked at his huge hand on the wheel. "I'd forgotten. We can do something else if you want."

He placed his free hand on mine. "I want you to relax. Besides, it's fun seeing you get all fired up."

SUNDAY MORNING, I groaned as the alarm went off. Titan had stayed until one, perfectly content to watch me play games the entire time, then he'd headed back to the cabin he'd booked.

Vera had texted to see if I wanted to drop in before I headed to church, since she and Neva had made too many lemon blueberry scones. As I walked into her yard, I was pleased to see Doctor Schneider and Lena coming toward me, hand in hand. The psychologist was carrying a brown paper bag. "Vera offered to give us some scones," he said jovially. "We met her daughter, too."

"Isn't she nice?" I asked. "I was heading over for some scones, too."

Lena gave me an uninhibited smile, and the doctor's gaze riveted to his wife, as if she were some kind of other-worldly siren. Apparently, her faith in the relationship had been completely restored. "It's good to see Vera get past this book club fiasco," Lena said. "I, for one, plan to step in and lead book club next time. I might even have it at my house, so Vera doesn't have unpleasant flashbacks."

"I think that would be wonderful," I said. "It was good to see you all."

I made my way up the stairs and knocked, triggering Waffles to start barking in the back yard. "I'm coming," Vera sang out, then she threw the door open. She pulled me into a hug.

The warm house smelled like baked bread, and the Christmas lights were blazing. Neva walked out of the kitchen, dusting off her apron. "Macy," she said. "It's so lovely to see you again. Let me bag up some scones for you."

As Vera walked me into the living room, I asked if Charlie had contacted her. "He did," she said. "First thing this morning. But thank you for texting me last night that Randall was in the clear. It was perfect timing, since I'd wanted Neva to get to know him a little."

"He's a good man," Neva said, handing me a paper bag. "I'm glad he can be here for Mom." She gave me an intense look. "And Macy, I'm so glad you're here for her, too. Someday, I wish I could move closer, but for now, I have to stay in Arizona and run my shop. I'm trying to talk Mom into flying out to visit, though."

Vera took my hand. "Maybe you could come with me, dear. I wouldn't be any good at flying alone."

"Maybe I will," I said. "Thanks for coming in, Neva. I know she needed you. I was getting a little worried about her heart." I turned to Vera. "Did you get in with Doctor Stokes?"

Vera sighed. "I did, even though I've been feeling much better. Neva's taking me over this week." She took a long look at her daughter, who was straightening an ornament on the tree. "It's turned into a wonderful Christmas, after all."

I grinned. "Well, I have a bit of news that's going to make your Christmas even brighter."

She gasped and grabbed my hand. "Did you and Titan get engaged?"

I chuckled. "Not quite. But Bo and Summer did."

Vera hooted and slapped her thigh. "Well, if that isn't just the bee's knees! How perfect! You tell Bo and Summer I said congratulations." She grinned. "And have your Titan stop by when he's in, too."

As was his Sunday morning custom, Bo dropped by to pick me up for church. Titan had decided to get some extra sleep, since he wouldn't get much when he joined his family for Christmas.

Bo rapped on my door. When I opened it, he said, "Thanks for the flowers, sis."

"What do you mean?" I pulled the door closed behind me and locked it.

"You know, the pink daisies or whatever they're called. The bouquet that was dropped off on the porch last night."

"Last night? Flower delivery trucks around here don't run at night," I said.

Bo's eyes narrowed. "Wait—if you didn't send those, who did? Who else knew we got engaged? That doesn't sound like something Titan would set up."

"No, it doesn't." I glanced at my phone. "We have a couple of minutes—show me this bouquet."

He jogged over to his house and returned, carrying a beautiful cut bouquet of hot pink and orange gerbera daisies that he'd hastily shoved in a vase. "I certainly didn't send those," I said. "Why would I send you pink flowers?"

He glanced at the paper still wrapped around the daisies. "I didn't think of that," he said. "Maybe there's a note."

Rustling through the green paper, he extracted a small card. "I should've noticed this."

I shook my head. "You were too excited to think about it."

He read it aloud. "Congratulations on your new position, Mayor Hatfield. I expect big things from you." He stopped short. "Macy, it's signed A.L.M."

"Anne Louise Moreau," I whispered.

We stared at each other, too shocked to speak. Whatever the crime lord's wife expected from Bo, it couldn't be good.

ALSO BY HEATHER DAY GILBERT

You can now preorder Heather Day Gilbert's
next Barks & Beans Cafe cozy mystery,
SHADE GROWN

**Welcome to the Barks & Beans Cafe, a quaint place where
folks pet shelter dogs while enjoying a cup of java...and where
murder sometimes pays a visit.**

During Lewisburg's popular summer home and garden tour,
Macy and her brother Bo discover new aspects of their
hometown's history. One of the last homes they visit features a
lush commemorative shade garden marking where a Civil War

soldier's bones were buried. As Macy pauses to admire a bed of blue hostas, she glimpses a shadowy shape lying beneath the dinner-plate leaves. It turns out to be the body of famed movie star Cody Franklin, who'd purchased the garden house as a quiet country retreat.

Back at the Barks & Beans Cafe, Macy speaks with Cody's distraught sister, who lets slip that she's afraid her brother's killer will target her next. Macy's heart goes out to the bereaved sibling, and she agrees to

speak with some of Cody's local acquaintances in hopes she'll uncover some helpful backstory.

But someone powerful is lurking behind the scenes, and Macy has to zoom in on the killer before everything fades to black.

Join siblings Macy and Bo Hatfield as they sniff out crimes in their hometown...with plenty of dogs along for the ride! The Barks & Beans Cafe cozy mystery series features a small town, an amateur sleuth, and no swearing or graphic scenes. Find all the books at heatherdaygilbert.com!

The Barks & Beans Cafe series in order:

Book 1: No Filter

Book 2: Iced Over

Book 3: Fair Trade

Book 4: Spilled Milk

Book 5: Trouble Brewing

Book 6: Cold Drip

Book 7: Roast Date

Book 8: Shade Grown

Be sure to sign up now for Heather's newsletter at **heatherdaygilbert.com** for updates, special deals, & giveaways!

And if you enjoyed this book, please be sure to leave a review at online book retailers and tell your friends!

Thank you!

Printed in Great Britain
by Amazon

15340958R00103